# EXPOSING
## the groom

# *praise for*
# EXPOSING THE GROOM

Finally, a romantic-comedy that isn't afraid to be actually FUNNY. It reminded me of watching all of my favorite feel-good sitcoms mingled with just the right amount of romance.
**~NYT Bestselling Author Lauren Layne**

Exposing The Groom is quite the hysterical ride and you definitely don't want to miss it.
**~Courtney, Read-Love-Blog**

Rachel Van Dyken has hit it out of the park with this rockstar/failed wedding romantic comedy. From page one, I was hooked. But then the jokes started coming along with the innuendoes, the snark, the characters, the once in a lifetime love. It was beautiful, and riveting, and I didn't stop reading from the moment I started until I finished the last chapter.
**~Sherry, recommendedromance**

Exposing the Groom is such a phenomenal romcom. This has to be one of my favorite romcom's yet.
**~Becky Wise, Goodreads Reviewer**

I don't usually do re-reads. Actually, I never have but I know when I need to laugh I will read this again. And again and again. Thank you, Rachel for the laughs!

~**Sandra Shipman, Two Book Pushers**

This book is like no other…it was actually a refreshing twist on what I normally read…this would make a great movie (hint, hint ~wink, wink)!!!

~**Mom's Guilty Pleasure**

Exposing the groom has it all. it's the best rom-com ive ever read. It's heartwarming, heartbreaking, romantic, and laugh out loud hilarious.

~**Julie Workman-Bookaholic Sisters Blog**

This was one of the funniest laugh out loud books I have read in a long time! There were times I couldn't see the words from the tears of laugher.

~**Vaneece, Goodreads Reviewer**

This whole book was absolute perfection. I had not read a Rom-Com this great in a while and I definitely need it.

~**Vanessa Ramirez, @betweenrealityandfiction**

This book ranks at the top of the most hilarious books I've ever read!!! Rachel Van Dyken just knows how to torture your laughing muscles.

~**Romance Me**

This by far has to be the best rom com that Rachel has ever written! I don't think I've laughed so hard while reading a book.

~**Beth Knight, Goodreads Reviewer**

Exposing the Groom is the #1 Rom Com this year! I can't form the right words so JUST READ IT!! For real. Sit back. Laugh your butt off.

~**June, Goodreads Reviewer**

# EXPOSING *the groom*

EXposing The Groom
The EX Files
by Rachel Van Dyken
www.RachelVanDykenAuthor.com

EXPOSING THE GROOM
Copyright © 2023 RACHEL VAN DYKEN®
ISBN: 978-1-957700-37-3

Edited by Kay Springsteen and Jill Sava
Cover Design & Illustration by Jill Sava, Love Affair With Fiction
Interior Design & Illustration by Jill Sava, Love Affair With Fiction

# A NOTE ON CONTENT

Some of you like to know if there is anything in a book that may be difficult for you to read. Some real-life issues are discussed/portrayed within these pages.
If you would like to see what they are,
please flip to the very last page or scan the QR Code

CONTENT GUIDANCE

As always, thank you for reading!
Hugs

# DEDICATION

*To all my readers*
who've waited wayyyyy too long
for another RomCom.

*Brady & Rylee*
fly high beautiful people

*Sharyn & Fred*
our thoughts snd prayers are with you

during times of great sadness
I hope you find times to smile
the way these beautiful souls would want you to

# PROLOGUE

## Scarlett

I t will, one hundred percent, go down as the most viral moment of my life—not on purpose. I think it was pure, uncontrollable rage that pushed me down the aisle. My smile is perfection, cameras flash from all angles, blinding me as I walk. Everyone stares like I am living the absolute dream. I even believed it for a few seconds.

He smiles at me, my fiancé Rob—what kind of name is Rob anyway? The things that I remember are always dumb ones, like Rob was never the name of the hot guy in college, at least give me a Zane or a Jesse, but no, I chose Rob.

Rob is safe.

Rob is secure.

Rob is boring.

But boring is at least predictable, right?

Wrong.

So. Wrong.

I used to date Adrians and Dukes—Adrian was the one you never brought home to your parents in case they disown you for life because he was constantly causing trouble in school, and Duke, well, he was actually British and so hot I introduced myself as Scar*wet* when I met him; he thought I did it on purpose. I've never been more mortified. I guess there's always room for more embarrassing moments. Lucky me.

Rob was in law school, came from money, had sandy brown hair, crystal blue eyes, a sharp jawline, and no joke, a country club membership at age fifteen. The guy was probably born with golf clubs in his hands. But I digress.

I'd like to point out I never ever thought about cheating on him, not once.

Not even when I got tired of missionary and asked if he'd pull my hair, only to have him say he was concerned that something was wrong with me.

"Women belong in a certain place, Scar, and you're so classy, how could I possibly do that to you? Let me just hold you, you're my treasure."

Oh yeah, he'd said treasure, and the idiot that I am, I melted like, OMG this guy is the best, while in the back of my head, I was like but what's so bad with being a little dirty? A little bad, like I was with the other boyfriends? And who the hell uses the word treasure? Is my hoo-ha a blushing flower on top of it?

He'd proposed months after we both graduated college, and I just let both moms take over what was supposed to be the wedding of the century between two of Seattle's richest and most elite families—which by the way, mine was rising on the way to the top and it was made even easier when the great Rob Danish the Third gave us instant access to his lifestyle.

I still remember going into the Everett Country Club and nearly passing out after using the bathroom. It had perfume, like actual perfume for you to spray down your shirt so your boobs smell like heaven. And not the Walgreens brand I kept grabbing because it was convenient and, in my opinion, smelled identical. No, they had Gucci, Prada— they had everything and mints that probably cost more than my Nordstrom Rack purse, my parents were worth a lot of money but they always kept us humble and never really exposed us to the other side of life.

I take another step toward Rob.

He smiles like I am his world, his eyes blurry with tears.

My heart sinks, knowing that it is all a lie.

I'd been lying in bed all night staring up at the fancy ceiling with its intricate designs and moldings and wondering if I could really do it.

My family will be disappointed if I don't. This is a whole new world for us. It opened doors that we could have never possibly dreamed of, despite our success. Plus, my dad has a startup that Rob's family already funded.

My sister is obsessed with her new big "bro."

He calls her Sprite and buys her expensive purses, so of course she loves him.

Should have seen that coming when he asked what kind of dog I wanted to adopt in order to prepare for the brood we would have later. Yeah, he said that to my face while she was walking around with a Birkin bag, but according to him, it was refreshing that I didn't need those things.

Listen, though, just because I don't need them, doesn't

mean I don't want them or would say no to an exclusive Hermes scarf just so I could rub it up and down my body. That's just science!

Tears flow down my cheeks as I take another two steps toward my father at the end of the aisle. He's softly crying, his tears mixing in with his trim white beard. He's wearing a black suit with a gray vest and tie. He looks so handsome that I feel even more sick. He's just… so proud, but he has no idea where my thoughts are. Mom's standing proud in her chic silver gown and matching tuxedo jacket, and she already has the tissues out, dabbing lightly so as to not mess up her makeup.

Everything looks like a fairy tale. A dream come true. My dress is pure silk with a shorter lace train in an intricate Beauty and the Beast design on the back because Rob remembered how much I love books. He had the designer flown in from Paris to hand deliver the surprise.

My fairy tale, and the first expensive gift he ever gave me. Truly, he went all out, he always goes all out.

How did this happen, then?

More tears flow. My makeup is going to start streaking if I don't do something, but all I can do is stare straight ahead and see flashes of my future.

Perfection.

With this man by my side.

This man who's currently smiling at me like I'm the Belle to his Beast turned Prince.

Maybe I watched too much Disney growing up.

Because I fell.

I fell so hard.

It doesn't matter that the sex is sometimes boring because

he is always there for me, he listens to me, truly listens. He cares, and as pretentious as he can sometimes be, he always apologizes and asks for my take on things.

Everything he gave me, I took for face value—when I shouldn't have.

Tale as old as time, am I right?

I can still see the text messages and the way my phone burned through my palm as I read through them, saw picture and video proof and just numbly got up and said I was calling it a night at my rehearsal dinner.

He'll never know all the goodbyes I rehearsed in my head, nor will he ever understand how hard it's going to be.

Stay or go.

My heart says stay.

My brain says run.

I wish I had Nikes on instead of shoes that cost more than my first car.

The music stops as my dad turns to me and smiles, his eyes crinkle, his teeth are straight and white, he literally cannot stop smiling at me as tears collect in his beard. I want to ask for help.

I feel so trapped I can't breathe.

And then the clenched, "I'm so proud of you, baby."

Another hot tear runs down my cheek and falls onto the gorgeous bouquet of white roses.

How perfectly pretty.

"Love you, Dad," I whisper.

He frowns a bit, then forces his smile back and leans in, whispering, "Are you okay?"

My eyes search his. He's aging. He needs this deal. Will they really withhold their support, drop him because of me?

I have seconds, not minutes. I give a small nod, then wrap my arms around his older and frailer body. "You're my hero."

He doesn't so much as hesitate before he whispers, "You're mine."

Strange, how people who truly love you and value you give you strength you never knew you were lacking until that moment in time.

"Who gives this woman?" the priest asks, clearing his throat. I look up. I know that voice; I've heard it say some very dirty things. It's not the time to ask my dad why we hired my ex.

Adrian.

Who's smirking down at me in a way that reminds me of more than his voice. I almost yell that God sees all, but I don't. His eyes narrow in on me, then on the groom like he's trying to make the calculations. Is she in love? Or did she just sell out?

Maybe, if I was being honest with myself, it was a little bit of both at the time. It was safe. It was exciting and new, and he was kind and I'd dated enough jerks to last a lifetime.

Poor Adrian has no idea the hell I'm about to unleash. I slowly shake my head at him and lower my chin. His eyes narrow even further as my dad's boisterous voice fills the church. "Her mother and I do!"

I flinch.

Rob comes over and reaches for my hand, prying me away from my father. He even shakes my dad's hand with both of his, as if to show that he's this dominant thing when he's literally afraid of taking me against a wall.

I'm suddenly even more angry.

I'd planned for this moment.

I crumple the paper in my left hand, and as we go through the ceremony and get ready to say our vows, Rob turns to me. "I think about you every day, Scar." His crystal blue eyes tear up. "You're my everything, you're perfect, my best friend, everything I've looked for in a life partner. Remember the time we adopted that dog with the missing leg, and you said that sometimes you feel like something is missing in you? I think that something was me, I'm that something, we complete each other—"

The actual hell? Is he comparing me to Samson? My favorite and only dog that I will sic on him if he doesn't stop moving his mouth. Oh God, does he have spinach in his teeth? Am I just imagining horrible things so I feel better?

"You're my little Bun Bun."

And he just called me our shared dog's nickname.

At our wedding.

In front of five hundred friends and my ex. Cheers, everyone.

"So friendly, so willing to do anything to please, and so kind to everyone you meet. I feel like that's where our story started, and this is where it ends, with forever, us together forever. All because you said yes to become the future Mrs. Danish."

He must see something like murder flicker in my eyes because he momentarily drops my hands and then picks them up again. "I love you."

I grit my teeth.

"Scarlett?" Adrian looks over at me, his eyes amused. I mean, at least *try* to hide it! "You can read your vows now."

"Can I face the audience? It's really important they understand the depth of my love for Rob." I smile sweetly, which also causes Adrian's expression to fall like he knows there will be carnage and I will be bringing it.

"Oh, um sure," Adrian says under his breath. "I think that might be a blessing for a lot of people." Adrian clasps his hands together like he is about to start praying. I turn from Rob and smile at the crowd.

Everyone's smiling right back. I even get a few thumbs up and a hell of a lot of phones held high in the air as if to say, wow happy moment, do your thing, I'm here to record it all!

Oh. I. Will.

I unfold the small paper with perfectly manicured and trembling hands and started to read.

"Rob..." I look back at him quickly. "...this is for you. These words were so meaningful, they really helped change my life, so I want to say thank you for being so transparent..."

He frowns briefly and says, "That's beautiful, thank you—"

"Damn, I wish my fiancé knew how to act in bed," I say in a loud voice, while the crowd gasps. I keep reading. "You're so hot. Don't worry, I'll figure something out. She's just a wife, she's not like a mistress. You're so hot, so sexy. Can you come over tonight? Let me send you a dick pick. I know you love those, though let's be honest, it doesn't even fit in the phone, ha-ha."

I keep reading even though Rob reaches for me.

I jerk away from him just as I hear Adrian mutter, "God be with you, Amen." Under his breath.

"She doesn't know. Come on, she majored in communications, you don't even need college textbooks to ace those classes, plus she looks good and people love her.

She never even argues with me, also you know how your dad has networked with a lot of people our company wants to work with. Why do you think I like your backbone? You should come over; she's gone for the next hour." Tears stream down my cheeks. "No, I changed the sheets." My voice cracks on that one. They were sleeping in our bed. Our bed. "She'll never know you were even here. I even told the maid." I choke up again. "My mom knows, she caught me texting you on the other phone, but don't worry, baby, baby, I'll break up with her once we're together for a bit and say she wasn't who I thought she was. Then I'll marry you, my true love." I start full on sobbing, hot tears fall like molten lava down my face. "My one and only love." I shake. "My little Addison."

My. Little. Sister.

I drop the paper onto the floor and turn to him. His face is so pale he looks sick, his mom is bawling, and his dad's face is completely red. He jumps to his feet.

I shake my head. I can't even say any words, so I turn back toward the crowd, hold my head high and say, "Let's not waste a good party, I'll be at the reception drinking. Oh, and Addison…" I glare at my stunned sister, my maid of honor, in her beautiful flowing gold dress standing by my side, black mascara sliding down her cheeks. I hand her the bouquet. "Your groom's waiting."

I don't look back.

I walk with my head held high, straight to the bar at the reception right outside the venue and across the hall of the Grand Hotel. I order a double shot of Jack Daniels and then sit to watch the band rehearse.

Killian Stone is the infamous lead singer.

He's beautiful with wavy messy caramel-colored hair and green eyes that people always speculate are fake.

They're finishing up their soundcheck. The drummer and other guitarist get up and walk off stage. But the pop rock god is still there, strumming something, smiling down at his instrument.

I toss back my drink and walk toward him, stopping right in front of the stage.

He's lost in his strumming, then he stops and looks down at me. "Aren't you supposed to be getting married? I mean, you're in a…" He frowns. "…beautiful wedding dress. What happened, get cold feet?" He winks.

"Sing me a song," I answer, and then I burst into tears.

And that's how I went viral.

Not from my vows, which were spectacularly captured on TikTok, but because I begged one of the biggest singers in the world to sing.

And he did.

While holding my hand.

# ONE

## Killian

I don't really know what to do. She's in a fucking wedding dress standing in front of me bawling her eyes out, and all I can think is, her tears, they're so pretty, just like her skin, her dress. Is the guy insane? What the hell is going on? I was paid to play for what was supposed to be the biggest wedding of the year in Seattle, and everyone seems to be missing.

More tears roll down her cheeks.

They aren't the normal angry tears.

They're sad.

They hold something I want to grasp in my hand, something that makes me feel. I've been stuck in a rut for over two years, and this rich princess, at her own wedding, has tears for me, at least it feels that way even though I know they're for her.

I still want to keep them though.

I reach down and slide my finger over her left cheek. She looks up at me, deep brown eyes, slim nose, firm jaw, and long lashes, and pretty blonde hair.

"Sing for me." Her voice is lower than I expect; it moves me, it harmonizes with my senses in a way I can't explain. As an artist, that's not something that typically happens so randomly, and yet I still stare at her. I hold on to her tear as long as I can before it evaporates into thin air.

I want.

I want more than anything.

I'm too shocked to move at first. I'm surrounded by beautiful women constantly... they only cry because they want me—not because they need me, not because they need my music, at least that's the way it always feels.

She doesn't know my past.

I know nothing of her future.

But we do have this song.

And it's one I'll sing just for her.

Maybe, in hindsight, I should look for cameras, or ask my manager if it is okay to go rogue, but all that seems to matter is stopping her tears, and giving her hope while at the same time, staring into her eyes with the realization that maybe it isn't *she* who is lost or sad.

Maybe.

It's me.

# TWO

## Scarlett

I can't take my eyes off him. He is strikingly beautiful. Even his hair is thick and unreal up close. I can't tell if he's wearing eyeliner, but his eyes are truly lined, making the green pop out so much I can't stop staring.

I can barely see through the tears streaming down my face when he leans down, grabs my hand, and effortlessly lifts me onto the stage.

A few people start to slowly trickle into the reception—all of them are watching me with Killian, probably wondering what the hell I'm doing.

Wish I knew! I just wanted comfort. A song. A hug maybe? Possibly another drink.

I know they're watching.

But I paid for this damn wedding, not the stupid cheater who's going to reap the benefits of free champagne, so why not get crooned to by the bad boy?

I know he quit his pop boy band four years ago—one of the biggest UK bands in the world—and I know he's gone quiet and has silently done some stuff on the scene.

To even get him to play at my wedding cost us over two hundred thousand dollars, for two hours mind you, but my dad used to be in the industry so he told me that it wouldn't be that hard as long as we forked out the money, which we clearly did.

And now here I am, staring into Killian's light green eyes, wondering what I ever saw in that other jackass in the first place.

He told me he loved me, and he lied. It's as simple as that. He told me that we'd be forever, and he gave me a small moment.

I feel like the girl who got the crumbs when all along my sister got the main feast. I was just the stand-in for what he really wanted, the person who would fall for anything apparently, to get his foot in the door when all he really wanted was my sister and me as a sidepiece while I popped out kids and took care of our dog.

What? Did he think he'd just stay married to me and have her on the side while my dad shares his contacts and works with his company?

Are men really that dumb?

I am suddenly so angry all over again. I can barely concentrate while Killian sings, even though his voice is like velvet. He reaches for my hand, and suddenly his voice grows sharper, cutting me like a knife, making me bleed, bruise, and worse, making me feel something I didn't feel at that altar.

Not just free.

But seen.

His hypnotic green eyes lock me in place. They're filled with secrets, and my tears start to dry. He tilts my chin with his fingers, such a light caress that I almost don't feel it, or maybe I wouldn't if I didn't feel the burn in his gaze.

His brown messy hair is framed around his face like he hasn't stopped running his fingers through it. Tattoos peek out from his neck and chest, all the way down his arms. Even in T-shirt and trousers, he looks like the rebel you never take home but secretly always wanted to just to prove to everyone in high school that you won.

He pulls the microphone away just briefly and whispers in my ear. "What happened? Anything I should be aware of? Like angry moms, dads who swear a lot and throw things? Or a groom that might attempt to castrate me?"

The music continues in the background.

I sigh and whisper back, telling the truth. "He cheated on me with my sister. I found out last night, so I decided to read his texts to her as my vows."

Killian's smile is wicked. It's breathtaking… straight white teeth, two dimples, all wrapped up in mischief. "Downright savage of you."

"They used our bed," I say through clenched teeth. "And he was going to keep her on the side. Did I mention he compared me to our dog in his vows?"

Killian bursts out laughing, then runs a finger under my eye like I've missed more tears. "He's an idiot."

"Thanks for saying that, but after today, it's going to be everywhere. I just don't care anymore."

"Well, then…" He looks over my head. "…if you're already screwed. Let's give them something to really talk about."

I have no time to protest. One minute we're having a casual conversation on stage in front of wedding guests, the next, his mouth slams into mine. He tastes like cinnamon gum. I reach for his biceps and hold on tight, then slide my arms up and around his neck. It's not a complete mystery why. He's hot, and he's kissing me, making it better. I am in a complete trance when he slightly pulls back, smiles against my lips, and says, dangerously close to the microphone. "Bet he never kissed you like that."

"No." My body is shaking. "He didn't."

"He's a dumbass," Killian says, but not to me, to the entire room, with the mic pressed against the mouth I just kissed. "Guess that means it's my lucky day... wedding dress girl. Wanna leave the party and have one of our own?"

My eyes widen. Does he mean it?

He leans in. "This will make him shit his pants, plus I promise, nothing kinky."

"What if I want kinky?" I ask.

He lifts my chin and nips my lower lip. "What the bride wants, the bride fucking gets."

# THREE

## Scarlett

I must be hearing things.

Did he just ask me to leave with him? And did I actually taunt him and basically beg him to take me to a hotel room?

My mouth gapes open like I can't believe what I just said, or um, his response.

He shuts my mouth with his thumb and winks, then leans down and whispers again, "He's right behind you. Choose your words carefully, because I'm sure it's already being live streamed somewhere." He bends closer, nuzzling into my neck, and presses a kiss there. "Your choice, always your choice, or I can stay and just mess with his head while I serenade you on stage for two straight hours." His brow furrows. "Also, question, what right does he have to look so pissed? He's doing this weird sucking his lips thing."

I cover my mouth with my hand and laugh. "Oh, that's his intimidating face."

"You have got to be shitting me. Shit, his head might just pop right off. Think I could kick and yell goal? Blame it on the whole British boy in America?"

More chuckles and giggles slip out until I'm laughing so hard I probably look like a lunatic, the wetness of tears in my eyes long forgotten. "I think I like you."

"I'm extremely likeable. Ask my fan groups."

"Oh, and arrogant?"

"We're the best type." He winks, then brings the mic back up to his face again. "So, what do you say, Scarlett? Wanna take off? Go have some real fun and let the groom enjoy his time with your sister?" He grins. "Cheers to the happy couple! May you never go to a wedding and find out that your significant other's been fucking with your family behind your back." He shakes his head and then adds, "A dog in the vows, bruh? Really?"

Killian quickly releases me, grabs his guitar from around his neck, sets it down, and takes my hand.

I glance over my shoulder. The groomsmen, my sister, my mom, and basically the entire wedding party are standing on the right side of the stage. The only people who seem truly ready to kill me are Rob and his dad. My dad, however, lifts his glass toward me and nods.

Rob takes a step forward, only for his dad to hold him back and mine to move past them. Well, shove past them was more like it.

As he approaches us, I wait for a lecture. Instead, he holds out his hand to Killian. "Thank you for coming. Sorry for the shitshow."

"Well, if I get a date out of it, I'll call it a win." Killian flashes a wide grin as the two shake hands. "She looks too pretty in that dress not to be seen today, and not just by people holding up their phones and gossiping."

My dad nods. "She's everything. She likes cookie dough ice cream and the little French cafe down on the pier next to the aquarium."

"Cookie dough, see? Match made in heaven." Killian grins down at me. "What do you say, runaway bride? You in for a date night to take your mind off the chaos?" He leans in. "Quick reminder, everyone needs chaos every once in a while, but it's healthy to cancel the noise and breathe."

"Yes." Is that me nodding like I'm not even in control of my body anymore? What is happening? "Yes. I'll go on a date with you."

Dad pulls me in for a hug. "Go have fun, I'll take care of all of this." He glances around the huge venue for the reception. Everyone is holding their phones up high, whispering, mumbling, shoving toward the stage.

Just as I'm about to address the giant elephant in the venue, Killian drops the mic, wraps an arm around me, and presses a kiss right on my neck. "Let's go!"

If you've made it this far, you now know how I, Scarlett Winthrope, became entangled with one of the hottest rockstars in the world.

But that's not where our story ends.

Nope. It's truly just the beginning.

# FOUR

## Killian

**"G**round rules," I say once we're safely in the waiting black Escalade. It took a minute for my bodyguards to actually understand what was going on and why I wasn't at the venue playing like I promised. My bandmates stayed behind to keep playing; they were new to me anyway, hired by my new label, and I'd only practiced with them a few times.

Shit. A wedding. How far had I fallen? And while the money was incredible, there was just something about going from selling out stadiums across the world to singing at a wedding reception in a suit.

My old bandmates—the ones that pretty much would fight each other for a chance to torture me, then murder me—would laugh their asses off.

As if I'm the one who made us disband because I had creative differences. The lie is always more interesting than

the truth, right? Shit, I had people camped outside my apartment for a week after we disbanded, food thrown at me at Taco Bell—who the hell gets rid of a good chalupa? I mean, really, that's the question here.

I think my favorite was when a guy at a local coffee shop stopped mid-set, saw me grab a cup of coffee and literally say into the microphone. "Fuck you, Killian Stone!"

People clapped.

To say it's been a fun few years, well…

I shake the headache already forming at my temples and turn to the pretty girl sitting next to me. "Sorry, got lost in my thoughts. Ground rules: no pictures, no posting on social media, no—"

She claps a hand over my mouth and shakes her head. "I think I've had enough of social media for the day, enough gossip, and what makes you think I'm one of those weird fans who's gonna tattoo your signature on my ass? I mean, come on. Do I really want to be an old grandma someday with 'Killian' scrawled across my ass cheeks?"

"Depends." I laugh. "Are you a hot old grandma?"

"I will do yoga until the day I stop breathing, so yes." She wipes at her still wet cheeks. "And nobody needs someone else's name on their body unless it's already etched on their soul."

My mouth drops open. "Wow, we have a romantic inside that broken little chest, and I don't mean little as in…" I point at her breasts. "They're not little, and you know what? I'm gonna stop now."

"Good idea." She pats me on the leg and leans back against the leather seat, squeezing her eyes shut briefly before letting out a long sigh. Her profile is gorgeous, she's curvy in all the right places. Her dress is a form-fitting silk with a plunging neckline. She isn't wearing a necklace, but has giant diamond earring cuffs on both ears. Her hair has pieces of honey colors drawn through it like an artist wanted to add some color, and it's pulled back into a loose braid. Her makeup artist must work in the industry because, despite crying, this girl still looks beautiful. Even with some remnants of raccoon eyes.

"So." She sniffles and turns to me. "Now that we know I'm not going to post about you, you can just take me home. I think I need to just… relax for a bit. Thanks for getting me out of there. Really." She leans away from me and lightly taps the driver on the shoulder. "I live off of Lake Washington on twenty-seven Cobble Street Way."

I smile to myself. "Wow, we're in the same neighborhood."

"We are?" She frowns. "How would I not know that?"

I shrug. "Maybe you need to watch more TMZ?"

"Okay, guy who probably Googles himself." She laughs. "I'm busy."

"Ah, so was it the business that had that shit ex-fiancé going at it behind your back or was it the fact that—"

She glares.

"Bad timing, yup, reading the room or um car, yeah let's drop you off, but you have to let me in. I did promise you a good time."

Her mouth drops open. "I'm not sleeping with you!"

"WHAT!" I say loudly. "Damn it, my entire night is completely ruined now! I was going to invite myself in for a drink, pretend that I had to use the restroom, strip naked, then toss myself onto your bed with a red rose between my teeth. Fuck, and they say romance is dead."

She cracks a smile. "Sure way to get arrested."

"Ah, wouldn't that make good headlines…"

"The rose in the mouth is a little much." She nods. "And probably embarrassing to tell the nightly news, but maybe if you covered your small appendage with it, I might find the rose at least enticing."

"Shots. Fired." I laugh. "Wow! Don't ever judge a guy's dick within an hour of meeting him. That's just harsh, and it's cold outside."

"It's summer."

"Right, a cold summer night."

She raises an eyebrow. "It's seventy."

"The rain makes the air moist."

She scrunches up her nose. "I don't like that word."

"Wet." I lick my lips. "I'll use wet instead."

Her eyes move to my mouth as the SUV gets off the freeway and starts making its way through our neighborhood.

She gulps and looks down at her hands. "I'll admit wet is better."

"Wetter is better," I correct with a smirk.

She nudges me with her elbow. "Seriously, thank you. I had to get out of there."

"Everyone needs a rescue every once in a while, even if it's from some horribly talked about rockstar or—" I'm cut off when the car takes an abrupt turn to the right. She falls into my lap, her hand slams onto my dick. We both freeze. She looks down but must be in shock because she doesn't move her hand.

My hands grip her shoulders. Her eyes scream that she's horrified, but her hand screams something else entirely since it's still locked in place.

I smirk. "You know, if you needed to tap out, you could have just used your words…"

She jerks her hand away.

"It's Scarlett, right?" I grin and lean forward as the car pulls to a full stop. "Invite me in."

Her eyes dart away from mine, then behind me like she's looking for an escape. Well, I tried.

She reaches for my arm and squeezes it. "Just don't upset the dog."

"The dog," I repeat. "How would I upset the dog?"

"He's half-blind, so he gets really freaked out with new people, and I don't have any meat for you to give him to tame him."

I laugh. "Oh, I've got meat—Son of a bitch, I need to stop talking, no more sexual innuendo, I won't scare the dog. Any more pets I should worry about?"

"Chuck Norris." She nods. "But he's in his tank, so he should be fine."

"Um, why would a fish not be in its tank? Do you have walking fish? And if you do, science has done us wrong, on an unfathomable scale."

"Turtle." She laughs lightly. "He's a red-eared slider and I take him for walks if you must know." She reaches for the car door, but I grab her wrist and pull her back. I really want to go inside, but I also really like talking with her. It's the first time I've had a decent conversation that hasn't given me a headache in the last few years.

"Can we revisit turtle walking?" I inquire, genuinely wondering who the hell walks their freaking turtle.

"I thought you wanted to go in." She starts to tug away, and the moon hits her cheek just right and I'm spellbound.

This is my moment. If I let her go, I may not be able to follow, she may lose her nerve, I may lose mine, and I really don't want this strange conversation to end.

I gently pull her back. "You drive a hard bargain, but I'm curious by nature. How does one take a turtle for a walk? Do you have a leash? Does he need one? Why Chuck Norris? What about predators? The sun? Snow? His all around slowness? I have so many questions. Do you have a rabbit too? Do they race? Is it legal to bet on it?"

Her laugh is infectious. She pulls her arm away and manages to somehow stare down at me like I'm the smaller one in that back seat. "Are you more interested in Chuck Norris than me?"

"Man's a legend, so absolutely one hundred percent yes. Sorry, we had a good run, but I'm gonna have to go check out my new best friend." I start to get out of the car.

"Wow, and I thought things were going so well." She sighs.

"Yes, I especially liked the part where you shook hands with my dick, super classy, might need to revisit that too," I call over my shoulder.

She punches me in the arm lightly. "Seriously, don't scare Bruno."

"We don't talk about Brunooooo." I start singing as I hop out of the SUV and hold out my hand for her to come out the same side.

"Ha-ha, as if I haven't heard that before, and Bruno was the name of Cinderella's dog, so there." She sticks out her pink tongue, licking her bottom lip, and reaches her hand for mine. I'm still focused on the way her tongue slides past her lips.

I'm so tempted to grab it between my fingers just to shock her, but instead, I take a few steps back, letting her follow. "Our destiny awaits."

"Hmm, destiny?"

"Destiny," I answer.

You ever wonder how much power one single word can hold?

I thought I knew. I'm an artist, after all; words are what I do. They're what I wield; they may as well be my sword.

But I miscalculated the power just like I miscalculated every step that led me into her house.

Every laugh.

Every sigh.

Even the silence was grossly miscalculated.

The moments where two people know it's right but wrong at the same time, where the kisses feel more urgent and passionate than they should, like you've struck the perfect chord with another only to know the song has to end—it must.

The world paused that night.

And like passing ships, we continued on.

And lived for ourselves rather than each other.

I still think about the times I stopped walking toward the SUV.

The number of times I reached into my pocket and touched one of the stupid coaster party favors I'd found on her table when I left in the darkness.

Some things mean something because they can't help it.

Some things mean something because they must.

And some things you force yourself to look at as meaningless because if you truly acknowledged their truth—

then destiny, for sure, would find you. And not all of us are ready for the truth.

Some of us look at truth as the end of the fake reality you've been living, tossing you into the rawness of your existence.

And some of us would rather live outside of that because it's the only way we can survive.

# FIVE

*Scarlett*

*One Year Later*

The mail feels heavier today. My parents both won't stop calling me, my sister keeps trying to text me, snap me, ask if I'm on WeddingTok, whatever the hell that is.

And if one more person sends me an AARP membership ad via mail, I will set the building on fire.

All of it.

Gone.

Including the apartment PO boxes, which I know is technically a federal crime, because that's the post office, which really, they're to blame for delivering the mail in the first place!

I stare down at the box sitting on my coffee table.

Stare a bit harder.

It's sturdy. Didn't expect that from my sister. She's more of an "oh look, a dove just flew out of my wedding invite, kissed you on your cheek, blessed the next generation, then sang Leonard Cohen's Hallelujah all before dying a very poetic death across the invitation just to prove their devotion," kind of person.

Too far?

Maybe.

I don't even care anymore.

I kick the box with my foot, shoving it nearly off the coffee table.

I'm curious.

That's the problem. I want to know what's in it, I mean, I know it's a wedding invite because her million messages reminded me along with the save the dates and my parents begging us to reconcile.

But still.

A box?

It's in pretty white packaging, but when I open it, it's brown and cedar planked.

Is this a new thing? Wooden boxes?

"Ugh…" I flop onto the couch and kick my feet against it before finally looking at it like Pandora put a curse on it, forcing me to stare it down.

Chuck Norris, my turtle, who is already out for a walk across the floor, gently steps up onto my foot. I smile and set him on my lap.

Anxiety completely gone. I'm totally fine.

Ha-ha. Nope, just kidding.

I look down and groan.

A small little poop stains my white jogger pants, because

of course it does. He stretches his neck, I love on it with one finger as I look at the box. "We have no choice Chuck, we have to go in."

He closes his eyes. I get up and walk across the living room and set him back in his tank, then wash my hands and spot clean my pants before facing the box again.

"It's fine." I'm officially talking to myself out loud. "I mean, it's not like I don't know what's in it. I just have to rip the band aid right off. I don't mind pain, pain is fine, pain is life, it's normal, it's human." I aggressively snatch the box off the table and jerk open the top.

Inside is a bottle of Prosecco, cheese, crackers, and a small note with an address. "We're so excited to be celebrating this special day with you at Sagecliffe Winery by the beautiful Columbia River Gorge in Washington! If you simply scan the QR code, you can confirm your attendance along with your plus one. Accommodations will also be included in the link. Thank you for blessing this rare love."

I nearly vomit.

Rare love.

Rare? Love?

With shaking hands, I shove the box away and lean back on the couch. I don't know where it went wrong. Was it me settling? Was it me being blind to how he treated me?

And why am I blaming him when my sister was the one sleeping with him the entire time we were engaged? I saw the way she looked at him. It wasn't even hero worship; it was pure need, like she wanted what I had—the shinier toy? I just thought that it was great they got along.

I had no clue they got along that well.

Better than he and I did.

Tears threaten.

Nope. I'm over it. Totally over it.

I rest my head in my hands and try to fight the memories of that night away, which makes me think of him even more—not the ex-fiancé. He's not worth another thought.

No, I think about Killian. About stolen kisses in the dark, ice cream, laughing over wine, and the way he tasted. I think about how he held me when I cried again, and how he soothed my tears when I was silent with nothing but more kissing, touching.

He was.

Is.

He's.

Everywhere now.

So famous that even with my parents' money, I'm not so sure I could even be up to par. Imagine when Harry Styles left One Direction and went out on his own? That's Killian right now. Sold out world tours. Women and men throwing themselves at him, interviews everywhere, number one Billboard album, all two months after we connected.

I have his number, but I'm sure he's changed it by now.

There's no way. Besides, I was like this rockstar charity case.

I kick the table again when Bruno trots into the living room with his leash.

Slowly, I get up and rub his face. "Is it time?"

He sits obediently while I grab the leash and attach it to his collar. I shove my cell into my pocket, grab some doggy bags and my keys, and walk him out of the apartment. Normally I jog, but today, today I'm calling my best friend and bitching.

He's a man of God; he'll be fine.

Post wedding, my ex Adrian checked in on me and come to find out he really is a priest and a great one at that, he still has that smoldering look about him which probably accounts for the fact that half of his attendance is always women, he still gets offers to model, and I swear one day we're going to find out he secretly writes erotic novels, but whatever.

I put in my ear buds and call him once Bruno and I are on the street.

"You got it," he says; he doesn't even answer with a hi.

"What? Herpes? A million dollars? A high five? What did I get?" I grumble.

"Tell me you burned your own apartment down because you were so angry. I hope you took pictures because I'm working on my next sermon, and I really think that it would be beneficial to have visual imagery about sinning for the patrons."

I glare at the space in front of me. "I hate you sometimes."

"You love me, admit it."

"Well, now that I know you're a safe space."

"I'm always safe, so? No burning? No cursing? Did you throw the box? But most importantly, did Chuck Norris live through the trauma?"

"Chuck Norris is fine, thank you very much, and I did open the box and I didn't burn things down. I just thought of doing it. Damn, I'm so mad I could set *you* on fire right now!"

"I think it's frowned upon to light a man of the cloth on fire, but if we're in that sort of mood, then I'll go with it." He laughs. "Shit, I was so mad I pushed an old lady in the street and said, 'What? What's your game, bitch!' And then I threw her groceries all over the ground only to stomp on the one solitary apple that rolled out all before taking a giant bite out of it and chucking it toward the homeless. I didn't even say sorry. I'm a badass like that."

I laugh. "Wow, call the cops. You threw an apple."

"Okay, turtle killer."

"HE'S FINE!"

"He can't inhale smoke, Scarlett!" he yells back. "And when we dated, you killed your own goldfish because you thought putting the bowl on the heater would help him heal from his trauma."

"HE HATED SNOW!" I yell.

"SAYS WHO?"

"GOD!" I say quickly. "FIGHT ME!"

"Low blow."

"Yeah blow, tell me you miss—"

"Why are we friends again?"

"Because you witnessed me dump my fiancé at my own wedding and run off with a rockstar and end up on the news?"

He lets out a dreamy sigh. "Sometimes I still think about it like an Instagram reel you can't stop repeating over and over and over—"

"Yeah okay, special time *is over*." I'm so distracted, I nearly run into a stroller. "Shit, sorry!"

The mom laughs and waves me off. She's in a matching little blue sweat outfit and her little girl is holding a cracker in her hand and waves at me. She has curly dark hair and is sporting a pink Nike outfit with black shoes.

"She's beautiful." I gulp.

The mom slows the stroller. "Thank you. She takes after her dad, he's gorgeous and so is the little miracle here."

My throat swells up. "That's so sweet. Well, have a great day."

"You too!" She keeps walking, and I stand still.

Maybe that's the new metaphor for my life. Everything around me seems to be moving and I'm just… stagnate ever since the wedding. I still have my job. I have money. I have friends and a family who, for the most part, supports and loves me, but I feel isolated and lost.

I start to hyperventilate.

"Scar?" Adrian says into the phone. "Scar, you good?"

I nod to myself. "I'm coming over. I'm bringing donuts."

After dropping off Bruno and stopping at the donut shop on the corner, I'm at Adrian's house in less than thirty minutes.

I knock on the door like I'm trying to escape getting murdered.

He opens it up fast. His inky black hair is draped down over his face and he's wearing nothing but a white T-shirt and black shorts. Barefoot, looking as muscular as ever.

"Forgive me, Father." I shove the donuts toward him. "For I have sinned."

He grabs the box. "You're forgiven, child. Go forth in peace, unless you didn't grab me chocolate. Then you're doomed to hell."

I gasp.

"Sorry." He holds up one hand. "I don't make the rules, plus you know I'm technically celibate by choice, right? I'm not blind. I'm considered a—"

I shake my head. "Not the time."

"Whatever, I could totally take a woman by the horns and—" He frowns. "I was so much better at dirty talk before the Bible."

"Song of Solomon," I offer up, taking a donut and stepping into the house. I make myself comfortable on one of his black leather couches.

"Her heavy breasts," he starts. "Yeah, I can't do it, I can't even read it. I'm probably the worst priest ever."

"Nah." I lick my fingers. "You're the best. Plus, you don't judge my donut addiction and you laugh when I curse."

His smile is friendly, easy. "You look like poo, by the way."

"Shit, it's shit, and thank you."

"I rarely curse. He hears all."

"So last night during the Cowboys game, you just slipped and had to go to confession yourself, or what?" I try to grab the chocolate donut, only to have him smack my hand, steal it, and sit on the couch.

"Football's holy, everyone knows that. Doesn't count."

I smack him in the shoulder, then notice a piece of strawberry jelly on my fingers. I suck them dry and wink at him.

"You're an animal." He rubs his shoulder. "Are we doing spaghetti night tonight?"

"Yup." I hop back to my feet. "After I'm done doing the ever lovely relationship podcast."

His snicker isn't at all helpful. "Perpetually single for the last year and still handing out advice... how does it feel?"

"It's mainly advice on sex, so there!" I stick out my tongue.

He shakes his head. "How's that working out for you? Didn't the last guy you took out in order to clear up the cobwebs end up asking you to play Legos during your date, then want to introduce you to his mom? Who was also at the same restaurant watching."

"She was protective." I sniffed.

"She had a Polaroid."

"Shhhhh." I clap a hand over his mouth. "No more memories of that fateful night."

He grins against my hand as I pull it away and pat him on the head. "Thank you for your wise counsel, as always. I'm off to go talk about all the sex I'm not having. You should probably go work on your sermon for Sunday."

Adrian's smile spreads across his face. "Fine. Go talk about sex while I go write about the ten commandments. Isn't there one in there that says—"

"I can't hear you!" I plug my ears and leave before he can remind me anymore about all the things I'm not doing while my sister marries the guy I was supposed to.

It doesn't take long for me to get back into my normal routine, i.e., pour a glass of wine and sit in front of my laptop and microphone to talk all things sex and relationships on my podcast. I guess the one great thing about going viral on TikTok and gaining tons of followers is that I could start a brand new career outside of event planning that includes things I actually want to talk about.

Until it starts reminding me of how single I actually am.

Or lonely.

Or sad.

At any rate, my new job at least provides for me outside of my parents' trust fund and allows me the freedom to do what I want.

So my ex can just go screw himself.

# SIX

## Scarlett

I stop counting after two drinks, and then I somehow manage to crawl into my attic, grab my sewing machine, pieces of cloth that are probably from curtains, and make a small tuxedo for Chuck Norris.

This is what it's come to.

I'm going to freaking bring my turtle to my sister's wedding.

"HA!" I laugh out loud and slam my drink back onto the counter as ice falls out. "You know what, though?" I point my finger at Chuck and sway with a double thumbs up. "Turtle power."

Did I just try to high five my red-eared slider?

My phone starts to ring.

I can barely see it, let alone grab it, but I manage to finally answer it only after horrifyingly realizing that I was texting earlier.

Wait.

Who did I text?

Leather Pants?

Who the hell is—

"Oh, SHIT!" I say, answering the call.

"Are you alive?" Adrian asks. "Weren't we doing spaghetti night? I've been waiting, and then suddenly no spaghetti and no Scarlett. And why did you curse? Are you even home? I listened to the podcast and then you haven't answered any texts for the last two hours, bro."

"Shit. Shit. SHIT!" I yell even louder.

"Use your words," Adrian says calmly. "In times like these, I usually—"

"I will literally rip your arm *off* your body, shove it *up* your ass and force you to say thank you if you keep talking!" I scream.

He's quiet and then, "That was extremely violent for a Thursday."

"Ha-ha!" I force the laugh out. "I'm fine, I'm totally fine, by the way."

"You're Fine? You're fine?" He sighs. "Tell me you didn't pull out the sewing machine again."

I look down at the sewing machine and Chuck Norris. "I was inspired, if you must know!"

He immediately requests FaceTime. I answer out of all my shame. He stares me down and then calmly says. "Show me Chuck."

"He died."

"Scar."

"He's busy! Turtles can be busy!"

"Show me the turtle."

Slowly, I lower the phone to add to my shame. Adrian sighs again. "Well, at least you did a really good job on the shell, can hardly tell he's a turtle and not a man."

"Thank you. I thought so—"

"Is that Celine Dion?"

Shit. "No! No, it's the radio!"

"You only listen to podcasts and Apple music. Shit, you literally have your turtle wrapped up in a homemade tuxedo and probably pulled out the Titanic blanket."

I guilty-look over at the Titanic blanket on the chair I was just sitting on, then drunkenly yell, "It sank, though! Jack died!"

"Duck me. Why are we friends?"

"Just say the real curse word, priest!"

"Wow, okay, so you really aren't good. Do I need more proof of life for Chuck, or should I just come over?"

"I texted Leather Pants."

"Oh, fuck."

"Now you say it!"

"Be right there, and whatever you do, *stop texting!* The Lord commands it!"

"I'm already going to hell for wishing hell on my sister and dressing Chuck Norris in a suit!"

"Tell me how was that the first option in all the bad choices you could have made, I'm truly curious."

"It was theatrical! For the TikTok!"

"FOR THE LAST TIME THERE IS NO *THE* BEFORE TIKTOK! IT'S JUST TIKTOK AND WHY DID YOU TEXT WHEN SAD?"

*"Stop yelling at me!"*

"Open the door," he grumbles.

Five minutes later, two knocks happen. I grab the door, look into his eyes that mirror my shame, and burst into tears. "I found the old pictures of the wedding, and the viral newspaper that I promised never to look at again, and it just all went to hell again!"

I sob into his shoulders. He hugs me tight. "So how much wine are we talking and what exactly did you say to Leather Pants?"

I sniffle and pull back. "I'm actually afraid to look."

He holds out his hand. "Give me the phone, I'll rip the band-aid off."

"No!"

I try to hold him, but he's too strong. He rushes by me, grabs my phone, points the wine bottle at Chuck.

"YOU DARE THREATEN HIM!"

"YOU DARE DRESS HIM?" he yells back. "You have to see how ashamed he is."

Why does Chuck choose that moment to twist his neck toward me in sadness, like he knows he looks stupid and knows I'm sad.

"Hi, Leather Pants, it's Adrian."

All goes quiet.

And I swear my soul actually leaves my body before I collapse onto the couch and put my hands over my head.

I'm such an idiot.

Such. An. Idiot.

I yawn. Such. An. Idiot.

# SEVEN

## Killian

**W**ow, of all the texts I expected to get, it was not one from the blast from the past.

She was so pretty, so perfect.

I wrote a song about her then refused to record it just because it was too personal, and now, she's sent me a crazy text of her turtle in what appears to be a homemade tuxedo, and a picture of her sister's wedding invitation.

Guilt slams hard.

But she doesn't even know why I said yes, why I felt compelled to say yes. It was all because of her. But saying that makes me look like the weak one, the one who walked away again, and the one who's always had regrets, wishing he could walk back.

The words to the text are a drunken slur.

My Scar
Be my plus one or immush taking Chucksh, and he's allergic to air!

I think it was meant to be a threat. I can't imagine she would kill her turtle, but what I'm more fixated on is the fact that her lean hands are pointing at the turtle and she has a pretty gold ring on her pointer finger that rests by her knuckle. Why is that so fascinating? Like her gray nail polish or the fact that she still has a sewing machine and chooses to use it on her pet?

The phone starts to ring, and I nearly drop it. She's calling now? She's never called me. Damn, all the times I've wanted to call her or send a text only to stop myself.

My PR firm didn't take kindly to our little stunt. I almost lost a record deal after "stealing" the bride. Thankfully, I turned it all around, but I was told to stay as far away from that nightmare as possible.

So I did.

I hated it. But I did.

But hey, one doesn't say no to a wedding invite, right?

That's the only way I can think of it without causing more drama now that my manager constantly checks my phone to make sure I'm still making the label money and living as the US version of Harry Styles.

No PDA. Easy.

No Drugs. Easier.

No Alcohol. Semi-hard.

No Sex. Also easy, because the only girl I can think of is currently dressing a fucking turtle and calling me on the phone.

"Scar?" I answer on the fourth ring.

"Hi, Leather Pants, it's Adrian," the male voice says. I nearly drop it like it's on fire and burn my own apartment down.

"I'm confused," I say. "Aren't you the ex-boyfriend? The priest? What, you get so tempted you quit the cloth for a piece of ass?"

"Ah, there's the rockstar, and you sounded so polite at first." He sighs. "And for your information, I'm still a priest. We aren't dating, but I am in best friend territory, especially on sad, sad nights like tonight where I find a turtle's been shamed."

"Is Chuck okay? I hear he gets anxious. Did you try the ground beef?"

He's quiet and then, "She told you about the ground beef."

I laugh. "Oh Adrian, I know all about the ground beef."

"It's sacred."

"It's his favorite."

"Just how much do you know Chuck?"

"Just how much do *you* know Chuck?"

"Why are we arguing over the turtle?"

"Same reason we're arguing over a drunken Scar, we care. She okay?" I sit on the couch and press a sweaty hand against my dark jeans. "I mean, I know invites got sent out. She just asked me to go but—"

"Oh, I know, you're busy, you're always busy, blah, blah, how did you even know it was her anyway?"

I know I'm too quiet. "Lucky guess when I saw Chuck."

"I can smell a lie from a mile away."

"Because you're a priest?"

His laugh is all sarcasm. "No, Leather Pants, it's because you hesitated. Must be the same choking thing that happened before."

Oh shit, did she tell him?

I lean back on the couch and curse, pulling the phone away from my face. "Seriously, is she okay? Can I talk to her?"

"Scar—"

He curses, then pops back on the phone. "She's already face planted on the couch and will probably have so many regrets in the morning I'm going to have to stay the night."

"You sure you're a priest?"

"I keep it in my pants, unlike some people. Job kind of requires it, faith adds to it, things that I know confuse the hell out of you, but don't worry, I'll say a prayer for you tonight. Think of it as a favor."

Who the hell is this guy? Seriously? What sort of priest talks like this? "Whatever man, just make sure Chuck gets back into his tank, make sure she has her blanket—"

"I know which one."

We're both quiet, and it's oddly not awkward. Finally, he sighs and says, "Don't go. I'll go instead. Just don't."

I know he's right, and I hate him for it.

"Promise me, Killian."

"You finally used my first name."

"It felt weird asking for a real promise from Leather Pants. Just don't go as her plus one, all right? I don't know if she can—I just, I didn't know it was like this, not until tonight. I mean, she talks sometimes about it, I know she has regrets, but sometimes girls don't want the knight in shining armor. They just dream about him when really all they need is a best friend and a shoulder to cry on and, well, someone to gossip with about all the wedding guests and throw slander at her sister. Don't worry, I'll ask for forgiveness later."

I smile. I hate that I like him. Stupid bastard. "Fine. Just tell her hi and I hope she's well. I mean it."

My heart damn near shatters in my chest when he says okay and hangs up. I drop my phone onto my desk only to have it ring again.

I quickly pick it up. "What now?"

"Ummm…" my manager Winnie says. "Rough night, Kill?"

"No, no, no." I shake my head even though she can't see it. "I just, never mind, I'm good. I thought you were someone else and didn't even look at my screen."

Huh, the power of a crush that refuses to go away.

Yeah, because that night was just me crushing on a woman.

I think back on us kissing on the couch, on the wine, the laughter, on her showing me her world, on me accepting it and needing it more than any drug in the world.

She had her sewing machine out and was making some cool Star Wars costume for Comic Con and showed me her podcast studio. I would have killed to be a guest and talk all things sex and love with that woman, then strip her naked and carry her into the adjoining bedroom.

"…anyway, it would be good PR since last time you actually stole the bride. God, what a nightmare, I'm still, whatever we won't talk about it, so what do you say?"

A swift panic hits me. "Can you, uh, repeat the first part?"

She sighs like she's already done with me. "Zane Andrews had to pull out of performing for the wedding because one of his cousins—the one who is rumored to be in the mafia—was hosting his daughter's wedding the same weekend and he had gotten the dates confused, so anyway. What do you say? One more wedding to redeem yourself from the last one?"

I want to say no. But now that I'm not a plus one and nearly lost to a fucking turtle, it was my turn to have a moment of weakness, just like Scar. "When is it?"

"Few weeks from now. You'll have time. It's at a winery outside of The Gorge, beautiful, has amazing places to stay, an on-site restaurant, bar, and it's known for its events."

"Fine." I sigh. "They must be paying a lot for me to just sing at the reception."

"Apparently, the bride's a huge fan and you were her first choice, but they weren't willing to pay enough of your fee."

"Fee? I have a fee?"

She snorts. "Ever since last time, we doubled it."

"Huh, so what am I worth now?"

"Half a million dollars for two hours of your time."

"That's like stealing."

"Remember my percentage." She laughs. "Okay, I'll book you and send you all of your information for your reservations. I won't be able to go with you to this one, so you'll be dealing with my assistant."

I groan. "You know how much I hate him. He's so dumb!"

"He just has no social skills."

"He tried to rescue a bird in the middle of LA traffic, then cried when the vet couldn't save its life only to find out that the bird was already dead. He fucking gave it CPR. Win!"

She laughs. "He just cares a lot, and he makes my life a lot easier. Just allow Dustin to be your right hand, he'll take care of everything."

"Right. Right." I roll my eyes. Dustin is like the epitome of someone who only has emotion toward animals and his computer games. Swear he nearly shit his pants when he found out Dungeons and Dragons was going to be made into a movie.

I heard he cried, but that's just a rumor—strongly enforced by his puffy eyes and red face an hour later in the office.

"All right, thanks." I hang up and stare back at my phone. She wouldn't answer anyway, she's passed out.

Because of me.

And what would I even say? Oh, by the way, I'm going to someone else's wedding to do what I couldn't do at yours? Let's finish what we started? I miss you?

I groan into my hands and groan even harder when my phone rings with the name Dustin on the screen. I swear if he wasn't from a loaded family who forced him to actually work, he'd volunteer at an iguana sanctuary and lead Ayahuasca retreats.

I don't answer.

So he texts.

Dustin
Yo, Kill, get it Kill? Cuz you slayyy the stage. Let's hook up tomorrow and go over details. I know a great place that serves some magical cruelty free Matcha.

I want to text back that plants are technically cruelty free *because...* they're plants. Instead, I just stare at the screen, shake my head and think that my year just got so much worse.

# EIGHT

## Scarlett

**"M**orning!" Adrian yells so loudly he probably gave me and everyone within a mile radius a concussion. "I'll have you know Chuck survived. I made you eggs. You have your next recording in six hours, and the dog already pooed but not in your apartment. I also did some tidying up. You really need to look into making your bed at some point this century. Oh, and Leather Pants says hi."

I jolt up and groan, then slowly lean back down on the couch. "I hate making my bed. Chuck better have survived, but he's slow enough I could have caught him. Thank you for taking out the dog, and he said what?"

"Hi and he hopes you're well and unfortunately he can't go as your plus one to the wedding."

"Oh, well." I slowly sit back up. "Of course he can't. I was just really drunk, and he's super busy. I'm just going to

take a shower then. Thanks for the eggs!"

I try to walk past him, but he grabs me by the arm and pulls me in for a tight hug. I relax against him. "Hey, don't worry. I'll go with you, all right? Who cares that I'm a priest, I'm still hot."

I laugh because he isn't wrong. "You're going to have every bridesmaid hitting on you."

"That makes me feel powerful." He kisses my forehead. "Now, get a shower. I'm gonna take off. You sure you're okay?"

"Of course I'm okay!" Why does it feel like I'm shouting while smiling? "I'm just hungover and feeling super stupid. Did you keep the tuxedo, though? I worked really hard on it."

"It shows, it shows." He nods, his smile doesn't quite reach his eyes, though. I know he knows I'm lying through my teeth, but he's being gracious enough to not say anything.

"Thank you." I close the door and then hear him leave the house. It doesn't take me long to walk to the bathroom, close the door, and slump to the cold white tiled floor and cry.

It's stupid.

I'm probably still drunk.

So why did I have hope that he'd say yes? Or that he even thought about me once or missed me?

It's better this way, and I have to tell myself that in order to get up and get ready for the day.

I'm happy.

So happy.

I have a great life, and I don't need Killian in it to fulfill any spaces, even the ones he left empty.

"You can do this Scar, you always bounce back. You always will." I get up to my feet by using the sink to stand and then press my hands against the porcelain sink, staring at myself in the mirror. My honey blonde hair is somehow sticking up like devil horns—I've always been a violent sleeper—and my lipstick is smudged.

Yeah, real winner right there, real winner.

I growl at myself in the mirror, then turn on the shower. It doesn't matter that I sent him an embarrassing text. He probably thought it was cute or dumb and didn't give it a second thought.

I strip and hop into the shower, then say to myself, "And now I get to go to my sister's wedding to my ex-fiancé, with an ex-boyfriend who they're going to think I sent into being a priest. Oh God, I'm Ross from Friends! I made him quit sex just like Ross made his wife a Lesbian!"

I scream for good measure and slam a hand against the tile wall and then repeat to myself out loud, "What's the worst that could happen? It's in a month, I have a month to get ready, find an amazing dress and focus on all the lies I'm going to have to say while staring at them in the face and saying, 'Congrats, I'm so happy for you two!'"

A tear slides down my cheek and then another.

It's not even that he cheated.

It's that my sister betrayed me first.

And they were going to just hide it, like I'm stupid, like I'm worthless, not worth a second thought.

It's the worst feeling ever, having no worth to others you hold in high esteem, especially when it's family.

I finish washing my hair and my hungover body and attempt to put on some makeup and a happy face.

I take Bruno for another walk and warm up Adrian's eggs for breakfast before checking up on Chuck Norris.

The sewing machine is still out, as is the forsaken tuxedo. I pick it up. "Gotta admit, Chuck, I did a pretty damn good job on this."

He crawls onto his floating bark in the tank and swirls toward me, stretching his head up like he wants it scratched.

I'm happy.

Totally happy.

I have Bruno and Chuck Norris. I have Adrian.

Now all I need is to get it together in the next few weeks, buy a hot dress, and pretend my heart still isn't a bit bruised and broken.

My phone goes off, shaking me out of my pity party.

It's my dad.

Again.

I know he wants us to reconcile. He's convinced that my sister's changed, that I would be so surprised and that she asks about me all the time, but I'm not buying it.

I quickly answer the phone. "Hey, Dad, what's up?"

He clears his throat. Oh no. He's about ready to make a serious speech. Growing up, my sister and I always knew that when Dad cleared his throat, it was time to make eye contact, stop fidgeting, nod our heads, and listen with such intensity that we would never forget the words of wisdom he was about to pass down.

Sometimes it felt like a listening test, or maybe a respect test, but he almost always ended his long talks with an equally long hug and, most of the time, ice cream.

"I'm worried about you." His voice sounds weaker than normal, not like the strong dad I'm used to. Is he crying? "I know you got the invite, I know you knew it was coming. Your mom and I really want you to make this work. Can you do it? For the family? For me?"

God, just slash open my chest with a butcher knife, grab my already broken heart, and squeeze, why don't you?

"Dad…" I barely prevent my voice from cracking. "You know I'd do anything for you. Of course I'm coming."

His exhale sounds like a million years' worth of stress just escaped his body. "Good, good, that's good. I just—we have to talk about some things in person anyway and I haven't seen you since Christmas."

"I've been busy." I hate lying to him, but I need time to heal and I know he knows me well enough to understand that space was included in that, especially since my sister still lived at home. Not that it's like she's in the basement; she has an entire floor to herself while she attempts to become a beauty influencer on social media.

I'm not one to judge, but she already has so much money and time on her hands it's baffling to me that she doesn't want to do something she's passionate about. She's never been interested in makeup tutorials, and the weird thing that always bothered me is that it almost feels like everything I did, everything I thought of, she decided she wanted to do.

Like my podcast? She decided months before my marriage that she should start one on beauty products. Okay fine, everyone's entitled to do their own thing, but then she opened up her own Instagram and kid you not, used the name AddyGal, knowing full well that my handle was ScarLady.

Mom said I was making a big deal out of nothing, but then Addison literally started posting on the same days I was posting, and the same content just with different colors.

I take a deep breath.

"Sorry Dad, when I say I've been busy I've just needed time to—"

"I know, honey, I know. I'm just happy you're coming to the wedding. Who are you bringing with you? Anyone in your life right now?"

"Oh, um…" I stare at Chuck. I swear he stares back at me with dread that he's going to have to man up and wear his homemade tux. "Um, actually yes, I am seeing someone, but he can't come. He has work and stuff, so I'm going to bring my friend Adrian."

"Your ex Adrian?"

"Yup."

"The priest?"

"Exactly." I force a laugh. "He's really been there for me, and well, if your priest suddenly has a heart attack or chokes on a shrimp, we have a standby!"

I slap my hand against my forehead.

"Well, um, sure." Dad chuckles. "Let's just make sure there are no shrimp nearby and we have a defibrillator."

"Good call, safety is always first." I nod like he can see me. "Anyway, it's going to be great!"

"You'll see, she's changed. We all have—for the better. Now, I'll let you get going. Oh, by the way, what does your new boyfriend do?"

The only thing I can think of is Hedge Funds or teaching, stupid, Zac Efron movie!

"He… he…" I panic and blurt out, "He works for a record label!"

"Wow!" Dad says. "That's incredible, that's a hard industry good for him!"

"Ha-ha, well yeah, he likes hard things!" I squeeze my eyes shut. Son of a bitch. I'm going to seriously end up in this apartment with nothing but a turtle, a dog with one blind eye, boxes and boxes of old newspapers, and they're going to find me buried underneath my Titanic blanket.

I'll be the modern-day Jack.

My heart will most definitely *not* go on.

"So, um, okay," he says, and I can tell I made it so very awkward. "I'll let you go. Love you little Scar."

"Love you too, Dad!" I force the cheerfulness, hang up, and collapse onto the couch. I find it hard to move, not because I'm stunned but because I have so much to do in such little time, and now I'm petrified Dad's going to tell everyone I have a boyfriend in the music industry.

"It's fine, it's fine," I tell myself. "Just explain to them that you broke up when you get to the wedding, fake a tear, everyone will feel sorry for you, then you'll drink copious amounts of champagne and lean on the priest."

Wow, even as I say it out loud, I want to walk into incoming traffic and wait for a bus to run me over.

Instead, I shoot to my feet, grab Bruno's leash, and call for him. "Let's go Bruno, it's time for our walk and our plotting."

And now I have Pinky and the Brain on my mind. "What are we going to do tonight, Brain? What we do every night, Pinky, try to take over the world!"

I don't realize I'm actually outside saying this out loud with my fist in the air until two high schoolers walk right by my apartment building and stop, then start snickering.

"Yeah, well!" I yell after them. "Laugh now because it's all downhill from here! Go enjoy your cafeteria lunch and making out after the football game because this," I say, pointing to myself, "is your future!"

They ignore me.

As they should.

Mr. Grenady, my neighbor, walks by me and tilts his head, then offers me a freshly unopened bagel. "I think you need this more than I do."

Tears threaten. "Yeah, I do."

I take it.

He smiles. "Things aren't always downhill after high school… have a good walk with Bruno and eat all of it!"

I nod and shove a bite into my mouth immediately, then with my mouth full say, "Thank you for the bread."

Yeah, you know you're in a rough place when you cry over a free bagel, but I'll take it. I eat it all, and I really do plot along the entire two-mile walk with Bruno.

If she's going to wear white.

I'm wearing off white.

And I'm going to buy an extra dress for every occasion listed.

I stop suddenly, nearly choking, and whisper, "With red heels."

# NINE

*Killian*

*One Month Later*

"**D**-Day!" Dustin adjusts his black-rimmed glasses at least five times with his sweaty little hands before checking his iPad again.

Swipe.

Swipe.

Swipe.

We've been in the SUV for maybe five minutes, and I'm already wondering if the child safety lock is on the doors and thinking about worst case PR scenarios if I jump out into oncoming traffic.

As Dustin continues to swipe, his facial expressions go from excitement to focus, then back to screaming excitement so that one might think he saw a boob.

Instead, I'm going to assume it was a picture of a

Stegosaurus or some dinosaur he's going to immediately feel the need to tell me about for the next hour as we drive from the Pasco airport to the winery.

For the love of God, please let it at least be a T-Rex; *that* would at least prevent my certain jumping from a moving vehicle.

"Wow!" He shakes his head like he just can't fucking believe it. "Did you know that the mouse has supersonic hearing? And they can fit through a hole the size of a pencil?"

Please don't take out a pencil, please don't take out a pencil.

And he's already reaching into his briefcase. He pulls a yellow number two pencil like he's Arthur with Excalibur and thrusts it into the air right in front of my face, nearly poking me in the eye in the process. "See! Can. You. Imagine?"

I stare at him. Hard. He has no ability to read the room. At all. I lean back in the seat of the SUV and sigh. "No, Dustin. I really. Cannot. POSSIBLY, fathom a mouse fitting through that pencil. So about the sched—"

"And, and!" He puts the pencil away and leans in. His shiny white teeth gleam in sharp contrast to his slicked-back, jet black hair. He'd be a good-looking guy if he just… didn't… speak.

Ever.

He's even wearing nice clothes, a calm baby blue T-shirt matched with some fitted jeans and black boots.

"And," he says a third time, like he can't even handle his own excitement over mice. "You can see their urine under a black light!"

And officially filing that under useless things I will never think of again.

"Wow, a hundred babies a year! Oh look, look!" Please

no. He thrusts the iPad into my face. "Their teeth grow longer every day."

I shove the iPad away. "Good for them. Say, shouldn't we go over the schedule? For the performance? For the wedding?"

"Oh, right, yeah, so…" He clears his throat and adjusts his glasses again. Swear on my nana's grave (Sorry Nana) if he does that one more time, I'm grabbing them and snapping them in half and feeding Dustin to the mice he so dearly loves. "Arrival in another hour once we stop to grab some snacks."

I frown. "Snacks? I don't need snacks."

"Me. For me." He sighs. "Low blood sugar, plus all the stress my cousin…" He shudders. "Anyway, we'll stop real quick, hydrate, grab some grub, then get back on the road. ETA, ninety minutes from now and then you can relax in your room, have a glass of wine, a bubble bath maybe—I do love those."

"Yeah, I bet," I mumble.

"Hmm?" He cups his ear.

I roll my eyes, a hundred bucks he has a stash of bath bombs with special prizes inside. "Yeah man, me too. Me too."

"Bro." He holds out his fist.

I bump it. I truly have no other choice at this point and right now I really need to get out of this fucking car. It pulls up to a nice-looking gas station surrounded by desert. A black SUV with blacked-out windows rolls in behind us, and I give a nod and a salute to the nameless, faceless bodyguards charged with keeping my expensive ass safe.

Perfect.

I rush out, open the door to the station, jumping slightly when it rings. It's relatively clean, has bathrooms you don't have to unlock to get into, and—I freeze.

They have burritos.

No, for real they have the gas station burritos, the real ones, not the ones you buy then heat up, the ones that have been cooking on a grill all day, most likely will give you food poisoning but are so crispy and delightful with just a hint of hot sauce that you just can't say no.

It's been years since I've had one.

I used to be so poor that it was my only meal a day trying to make it in LA. So there's a certain sort of nostalgia. Plus, I'm starving despite what I told Dustin, and it sounds so good I'm ready to eat it right now.

I walk aggressively toward it, and just when I'm about to grab it, a small feminine hand reaches out to touch it.

Cheese. Beans. Burned outside.

My. Burrito.

Hey, I recognize that hand! Those nails! Those—

"You!" I don't mean to yell it so loudly, but she did just touch my food and I'm weird about people touching my food.

Scarlett's eyes widen. "You?" She looks around. "Is this like some sort of hidden camera show or something?" She reaches for the burrito again.

I can't help it. I slap her hand away, and I'm weirdly satisfied that the burrito is unharmed.

"Excuse me!"

"Yes." I nod and cross my arms. "Excuse you, that's my burrito."

She cracks a smile. I tell myself it's not pretty. Because it's *not*. I'm not distracted. I'm solely focused on the food. "Oh um, did you put your name on it like all the good little boys do on their coats in first grade just in case they get lost or…"

I make a face. "No, I just I claimed it the minute I walked in."

She scrunches her nose. It's *not* cute. Really. "Gross, you peed on it?"

"NO!" I yell even louder. "It's the last one. I saw it, and you weren't even standing there. It's like you're a ghost appearing out of nowhere. Why are you here again? Holy shit, are you stalking me? Did the turtle tux send you into a downward spiral?" I'm genuinely concerned at this point. I mean, it's one thing to make a tux for your turtle, er, I guess, but to actually follow me to the remote small area that I'm about to go into? No. That's too hard core.

"Hey, hey…" I use a gentler tone. "There, there, are you lost? Does anyone know where you are? I mean, I didn't know it was this bad—"

Her nostrils flair, which means I stop talking immediately because I want to live. "I'll have you know I have no gas!"

"Well, that's a *you* problem." I smirk.

"Idiot, my rental needed gas, and I'm driving to my sister's wedding, and I've had a nightmare at the airport and hey, why the hell are you here? Are *you* stalking *me*?"

"Ha-ha." I wish. "No. I'm headed to…" My eyes narrow.

Her eyes mimic mine.

"Sagecliffe?" I offer.

She pales.

"Oh, shit." And yet I still reach for the burrito.

It's her turn to slap my hand away. I don't even know what to do other than pretend it didn't hurt and stare at her.

"Bride or groom?" I ask.

She rolls her eyes. "Did you even look at the invite?"

"I literally pay people to look for me."

She shakes her head slowly and reaches for the burrito again, then jerks her hand back when I glare. "It's my sister."

"The burrito?"

"The wedding. It's my sister's wedding."

Dumbfounded, I stare harder and attempt not to get lost in her green eyes. "Wait, at Sagecliffe? To—"

Scarlett looks down at the off-white tile floor, her eyelashes are so long I feel like I'm more lost in them than the deep green of her eyes. "Yeah, she's marrying… him."

Him. Rat bastard. I don't even want to say his name or think about him or him touching her, trying to marry her, sleeping with her sister, him.

Has there ever actually been a worse pronoun?

HIM?!

THAT GUY?

She waves her hand in front of my face. "Did you just have a stroke?"

"I'll stroke someone," I bite out.

Her eyes widen. "I don't think it's that kind of gas station."

I shake my head. "Never mind, so we're going to the same place."

"Yeah." She rocks back on her heels while I suddenly find the floor extremely interesting with its burrito grease and one long lost hair. "Cool."

"Yup."

"So I'm singing."

"Okay, Judas, just make sure to keep all that silver."

"Oh, please, you're going too!"

"Family."

"Friend!" Okay, she's not a friend, more like oh look money, that's my friend. "Whatever." I snatch the burrito and walk to the cash register, tap my card against the machine, and walk off. I should stay. I really should talk with her, but she's distracting, and weirdly aggressive with her communication. It's like she brought out the best in me when we first met, then decided to switch teams and bring out the worst.

By the time I'm in the limo, I can't even eat the burrito I was so excited about because she's leaving the gas station and getting into her rental.

Something hits my shoulder, nearly causing a calamity with the burrito and the sauce I grabbed. "What?"

"You okay?"

It's Dustin.

"What the hell? When did you even get in here?" I jerk my burrito away and stare at his perplexed face. When did he get glasses? Wait, has he always had glasses on? Am I losing my mind?

Dustin frowns, making his glasses slide down his nose in a way that has me annoyed for absolutely no reason. "Um, I've been waiting for you for like five minutes. I grabbed food, went to the bathroom, passed you twice, I even asked if you wanted water, but you were slapping some poor woman over the burrito I'm assuming is in your hand, and I told you I'd be waiting in the limo."

How did all of that just happen?

See! She makes me crazy! With her crazy turtle antics!

I shove the burrito into my mouth and take a bite. It's

crunchy, weirdly juicy, and I'm pretty sure I taste nothing but oil and extra grease, but it's worth it, because I got the burrito in the end.

"That sucks." Dustin points out the window. "Looks like her car isn't starting, and it's really hot out."

Don't look. Don't look.

I glance.

It's Scarlett, with the hood up to her tiny little rental car. She's pacing, probably cursing by the looks of it. Why does she have to look so sexy in her jean shorts and stupid white T-shirt?

And why the hell am I in such a bad mood?

"I mean…" Dustin won't stop talking. "She's probably going to be stuck there. Anyway, weren't you guys arguing in the gas station? Is she okay? Looked kinda crazy to me and really wanted that burrito—hey, can I have a bite?"

"No," I snap. "I don't share food."

He holds his hands up. "Just a question." His right hand goes to the roof. "Let's get on the road."

The driver starts the car. We're pulling out and right past her when I see her kick the tire.

And then.

The tear.

It was the tear that fell from her left cheek onto the cement that did it. "Stop the car!" I'm yelling, no idea why, other than I wanted our driver to hear us. Before I realize what I'm doing, I'm out of the limo and right next to her. "Hey, you need help?"

She rolls her eyes. "Oh perfect, a knight in shining armor, yes dear sir, please rescue me from my turmoil!"

"That was a weird voice, could have done better."

"It was on the spot." She sticks out her tongue. "Anyway, yes and no, it's a rental, so I have to call the company, and I still have to make it to the rehearsal dinner in the next few hours and as of right now I'm one burrito short of killing the next person who talks to me, so yeah, not so great."

"Where's the date?"

"Oh, you mean my sexless priest? He had to do a sermon for a school—or something. I don't know. Anyway, he doesn't get in until tomorrow."

"Oh."

"Yup."

"So you're stuck."

"Keen observation, yes."

The wind suddenly picks up, her hair glides across her face getting stuck in her pink lip gloss and truly all I want to do is tuck it back then see if her lips taste like candy since they're so pretty.

Shit, what is wrong with me?

She dressed a turtle!

I hear a car door slam and pray it's one of the bodyguards and not Dustin, but of course it's Dustin because, well, it's *Dustin*. "Hey, we gotta get going. Do you need a ride?"

No. She does not. She does *not* need a ride.

"Actually…" Scarlett looks up at me, peeking from behind gorgeous long lashes and an easy, wide smile. "I do, since we're going to the same place. What a gentleman."

"SHE DRESSED A TURTLE!" I don't know why I'm yelling this, or why other people are staring at me like I'm the crazy one, but I immediately want to die on the spot.

"He was fine!" she says under her breath.

"Yeah, okay, choking on his own bowtie. Oh wait, isn't

that what your ex was doing during your vows?"

"Take it back!" She grabs my arm.

I jerk away. "No, you take it back."

"Ha-ha," Dustin spreads his arms wide, "We're all friends here, let's just get in the car, avoid any sort of PR disaster, and get to the winery where we drink all the wine and forget about turtles, exes, and burritos."

She gasps. "Did you eat it all?"

"Oh no." Dustin holds out the burrito I left. "It's right here, if you're hungry you should just"—she takes it and literally annihilates half of it with one bite—"um inappropriately take advantage of it and digest without chewing."

I jerk it out of her hands and pop the rest of it into my mouth before climbing into the car and reaching for the bourbon. It's going to be a long drive.

She follows suit. Dustin looks paler than I've ever seen him, and somehow, we're suddenly on the road headed toward actual disaster, aka her sister's wedding to her ex-fiancé.

Cheers.

# TEN

## Scarlett

've never experienced such a need to choke someone in my entire life while also wanting to kiss the crap out of them and beg them to hold me tight.

That's Killian in a nutshell.

He's too pretty to harm.

His smile is too genuine to be fake, even when he probably *is* faking it.

He likes gas station burritos, damn him, and he's a betrayer of all betrayal going to my sister's wedding. How dumb is he? Maybe that's it. He's just dumb. I ask him to go with me and he says no, then on top of that he decides to go sing as if it's like wedding number two for him just with a different bride!

I shriek.

Dustin, the assistant next to me, jumps a bit, then scoots very far away from me like I'm minutes away from unaliving him, and Killian just smirks.

God did humanity a disservice with this one. He's freaking gorgeous, and I swear on all burritos everywhere he just gets better looking the more you stare, which I'm one hundred percent not doing.

No, I'm just awkwardly staring at my hands, wondering if my dresses will look pretty enough for the wedding and praying Adrian makes it in time for the morning, so I don't look like a complete loser.

"So—" Dustin's voice cracks. He's one of those, the type who gets nervous and can't control their tone. "Are you from the Seattle area or—"

"Small talk." Killian interrupts. "Don't waste your time, yes she is, yes she's pretty, yes she's—" His face suddenly pales.

Dustin leans forward and takes the glass of bourbon from his hand. "Are you okay? Are you sweating?"

"Um." Killian's stomach rumbles a bit. He touches it and coughs. "No, I'm good, bro, I'm good, just a bit car sick."

"Should you sit in the front?" Dustin asks. "We can pull over—"

"Oh, he's fine." I grin. "He just needs a minute to collect himself and—" Suddenly my stomach gets a shooting pain. I can both feel and hear it.

Killian locks eyes with me.

I cling to that lock like his stare will save my life.

This isn't good.

This doesn't feel good.

Our nostrils flair at the same time as we whisper, "The burrito."

Killian jumps for the door.

"We're still moving!" Dustin yells.

"GET US OUT!" I scream back at him. "YOU DON'T KNOW!"

"NOBODY SHOULD KNOW!" Killian screams. "Damn it! Stop the car!"

"S-stop the car!" Dustin hits the ceiling. "Stop the car!"

The car jolts to a stop, sending me careening backward onto the seat before I clamber toward the nearest door.

Killian scrambles out his door, I tumble out mine. Dustin looks ready to puke he's so nervous, but really all I'm nervous about is the fact that I clearly have food poisoning with a rockstar and the only solace I can have is that he does too.

"Don't look at me!" I yell, running off the side of the road in the opposite direction in search of a tree. At this point I don't even know what I can do to make it better. I just know that something died inside both of us, and we may not make it through.

"Knives," Killian yells. "It's the knives in my stomach, I'm not okay, are you okay? Don't look back, don't look back!"

"This is exactly how Jack died on the Titanic, Killian. He couldn't hold on!"

"But he TRIED!" Killian yells, his voice cracking at the end. "He tried!"

Killian disappears behind a tree and small hill and I nearly faceplant into a hole by a small rock in the desert before figuring out what I'm going to do with my life.

Really, I just want to know what happened? How did we get here? We got along so well and then he just left me.

*"Stay," I whispered. "Stay the night."*

*How was even his swallow sexy? The way he slowly leaned down and pressed a kiss to the corner of my mouth. He smelled* like every expensive cologne commercial I've ever experienced. Killian pressed his body against mine, smelling like wine and a future.

"I don't know if I should," he whispered. "We barely know each other."

"We know enough," I said. "I know you like turtles, I know you make your bed every day, which is adorable. I know you sometimes drink hot chocolate at three a.m. and pretend to be this hard core rockstar but would really prefer to be watching Dateline."

He laughed. "Okay, so my obsession with crime, you gotta take that to your grave."

"Done."

He pressed another kiss to my cheek. "I think I could fall for you, but I shouldn't."

"Why?"

"Because smart girls like you are dangerous to dumb guys like me. We get confused, in over our heads, we fight, we war, we brave everything just to have one small taste and I think you're the type I'd want to taste forever."

I had nothing.

Nothing to say to that other than kissing him, pressing my mouth against his and begging to drown in the words he just said.

He kissed me back—hard, pressed me up against the counter, then lifted me like it was nothing as his tongue dove into my mouth. His body felt primed, ready, muscular, and on top of that, his dick strained against his jeans, hot, needy. I'd never experienced something like that before, and then he just stopped.

He jerked away.

*His eyes were wide, his expression foreign. "I gotta go."*

*"Wait, what?" My lips were still bruised, my ego even more so. "Is everything okay?"*

*"Yeah, no, um I just forgot and…" He did a little spin, and then he was gone. I still had his number, but he left, just like that.*

*And there I was, left on the counter, sitting, just like that.*

*Waiting for him to change his mind.*

*To come back.*

*To tell me that he was just having a moment.*

*The car started.*

*And then he was just. Gone.*

I finally find a place to use as a restroom and am so thankful I have Kleenex and wipes and not nature at my service. It's suddenly not as bad as I thought. I'm not sure what Killian is going through, but I hope it's hell.

He abandoned me.

And tried to steal my food!

And then suffered for stealing it, but whatever.

I walk back to the limo and get in.

Killian gets in about a minute later.

We don't make eye contact.

"So." Dustin clears his throat. "Maybe we don't eat gas station burritos anymore, yeah?"

Killian groans and closes his eyes. "We talk about this never."

"Hey, you're still sexy." Dustin hits him on the stomach. Killian groans and looks ready to puke.

I hide my laugh, then groan myself when it hurts to make a noise.

"So uh, why do you guys hate each other?" Dustin asks. "I mean, I can read a room, and this one…" He makes a face. "More toxic than that burrito."

"He kissed me," I blurt. "And then left me as if it wasn't the best kiss of his life and mine. Just left without a word."

Killian is quick to respond. "She reminded me of someone I once knew, of someone who changed my life only to leave me."

I frown. "What?"

"Eighth grade, I did two semesters in the states. She was my first kiss. She had butterfly earrings and—"

"Always wore a bow in her hair?" I finish, ready to pass out.

"Her name was Letty."

A tear streams down my cheek. "Were you going by the name Len?"

He jumps forward out of his seat. "How do you know that?"

I hold out my hand. "Nice to see you again, Len. My nickname was Letty."

# ELEVEN

## Killian

'm too stunned to grab her hand. How did I not see it? And what are the odds? Damn it, that's why I've been so obsessed with her hands, they were familiar, pretty, small.

I gently take her hand in mine and narrow my eyes. "But your name's Scarlett."

She drops my hand. "I know my name. Once I hit sixteen, I wanted to sound more the adult I thought I was, so I told my parents to start calling me by my full name, then that eventually turned into Scar, which was a horrible choice since boys can be cruel and would chase me around singing the song from Lion King. One boy used to hiss at me." She crosses her arms.

"Did you kick him?" I ask.

"No, but I did push him against a locker once and tell him nobody was ever going to love him if he didn't use his words."

"Harsh."

"He's gay now." She nods. "And probably happier without me, let's be honest. Sometimes I stalk his Instagram."

I cough into my hand. "Shocker."

Not that it's a bad thing he's gay, just that I'm staring at a woman who quite literally might send others into other options.

"Oh, please. I didn't make him gay because I traumatized him over women." She rolls her eyes. "You would assume something like that. He just preferred P over V."

"If you say so." I grin. I know she's seconds away from arguing with me over something ridiculous again. At least we've moved past the burrito. God, how embarrassing, at least it attacked her too.

How would we ever be able to have sex after that?

Not that I'm thinking about sex.

Not that my dick is rubbing extra hard against my jeans ever since touching her hand like I really am back in middle school fawning over her.

"So," Dustin interrupts. "What's the story? You broke his heart?"

"He left," Scarlett says. "And back then there was this thing called AOL chat. I know, I know we're old." She saves off Dustin. "Anyway, I was heartbroken that he had to go back home, but he said he'd message me."

"I lost it," I finally say. "I lost the piece of paper with your handle on it, but I searched like crazy through all my stuff. Not that it matters because you had my handle and could have reached out too."

Dustin shifts uncomfortably between us and then reaches for the bourbon and a crystal glass. "Riveting, so you're saying you broke each other's hearts at fourteen and you fight over food now. Why don't you just thank the universe for meeting again, get drunk, go to your hotel room, and get rid of all the sexual tension? Gotta say it's really uncomfortable in here right now." He tugs at his collar again and forgets to pour the bourbon in the glass, just drinks it straight from the bottle.

"Ah, you make men gay, and I make them alcoholics." I snatch the empty glass from Dustin and hold it out. "Cheers."

She frowns, then reaches for her own glass. "If you get bourbon, I get bourbon."

"Sweetheart…" I purposely lower my voice to annoy her. "I'm not sure you can handle my bourbon."

Dustin chokes on his next sip and keeps on choking, pounding his chest while he's at it. Who thought it was a good idea to bring him again?

Scarlett slides her hand across my thigh and grips it, her fingers are dangerously close to my dick. "Wanna bet?"

I lean forward. "I bet you'd choke."

Her nostrils flare, damn she's pretty when she's pissed.

And I'm so turned on I'm ready to put headphones on Dustin and ask her just how far she's willing to go to prove a point.

Her tongue sneaks out and licks her lower lip, and you know it was completely on purpose to draw my attention to her mouth again and think about how nice it would be to taste.

Dustin interrupts our little moment and pours her two fingers of the bourbon. She swallows like a champ.

I'm not okay.

I lean forward.

Dustin moves between us.

I imagine kicking him in the dick when Scarlett's phone suddenly goes off. Who the hell doesn't have their phone on silent these days?

She cutely, or damn it, not cutely, puts her glass down between her feet; her white Converses hold it in place while she answers.

"Adrian!" Okay, but did she need to yell his name like he was giving her an orgasm through the phone while saving the world and holding Captain America's shield? Give me a fucking break! He's a priest! PRIEST! Am I going to hell for cursing and saying priest in the same sentence? I mean, technically, a priest would be worthy. Why am I putting him on the Avengers right now over one phone call? I glance over at Dustin, but he's riveted on the conversation going on and the way Scarlett keeps laughing into the phone.

She laughs easily with him.

And yet she mocks me with that same laugh when she's with me.

How did we go from wedding rescue to this?

I sulk, lean back against the seat and hold my glass out to Dustin, he shakily pours it to the rim on accident. Whatever. I drink it. Slowly.

And then suddenly it's gone, and I'm really feeling it. I haven't drunk in forever, I try not to make a habit out of it when I'm on tour and writing.

Scarlett laughs again. "Okay, well, as long as you make it in time for the bridal brunch." She rolls her eyes. "Wear board shorts and I'll murder you."

Board shorts? For real?

"Yeah…"

The hell? Is she twirling her hair? Does she like the eunuch?

"So technically…" Dustin clears his throat. "Priests aren't eunuchs."

"I said that out loud?" I glance over at Scarlett.

She just shakes her head at me like she's disappointed and confused. "Oh yeah, that was Leather Pants."

She pulls the phone away from her ear. "Stop yelling."

He's yelling? HE'S YELLING? What right does he have to yell?

She holds her phone out to me.

Shit.

I hold it to my ear. "H-hey, man."

"You promised."

My sigh is deep and full of self-regret. "Right, but this was booked for me, and I didn't know, and she had car trouble at the gas station. Should I have just abandoned her?"

"Yes! You abandon her. You call a tow truck and you get your dick far, far away from her heart."

I frown. "Do you really think that's how it works because you're a priest now or—"

"I had plenty of sex before becoming a priest, you jackass, I'm just saying, your dick probably would confuse her heart and—whatever. I don't need to explain. Do me another favor. The minute you get there, go your separate ways. My flight was delayed, but I'll be there in the morning and whatever you do, do not tell her about Chuck."

My entire body freezes. "Oh um, okay, so what happened with Hank?"

"Chuck."

"Code, man, code!"

"Sorry, I'm not a liar, so it's hard to pick up on specifics." Could his voice be any more patronizing? "Anyway, he escaped. I finally found him, but he'd gotten into my burrito."

Seriously, burritos are from Satan.

"The ugh, beef?"

"Exactly. I think he might have grabbed some cheese by the glisten on his shell, but again, I think he's good. The turtle sitter gets here in an hour and I'm gonna have her monitor him."

"You'll die if anything—"

"Shhh, it's fine. At least he's not at a wedding choking on champagne and watching you gyrate your hips, you heathen."

"Did we just time travel to the nineteen fifties?"

He's quiet for a minute. "Just... stay away. She's fragile."

I look up, and Scarlett is literally taking a straight shot of bourbon. "Yeah man, if you say so."

She doesn't even cough.

Damn girl, just damn.

"Why did you just start breathing heavy? Is your mouth open? Are you staring? Is she alive? And why aren't you responding?"

"How could I when you take up every single second I'd be able to, dumbass?" I pull the phone from my ear, then put it back. "And sure fine, whatever you say, dick and heart protected."

Scarlett finally starts coughing, Dustin hits her on the back.

I hand the phone over. "The celibate is all yours."

She makes a face, grabs the phone, and holds her glass out again. This will not end well; this will not end well at all.

She scrunches up her nose in a cute yet sexy way, and I'm ready to smile at her. Instead, I look away.

Adrian, what kind of priest is named Adrian anyway?

I can't imagine God's happy with this guy just… poking around everywhere and thinking lustful thoughts like the ones I'm thinking right now.

Son of a bitch, why does lipstick have to look pink sometimes? And why does she have to wear it? I'm a sucker for pink lipstick; it's both innocent and enticing but at the same time so light that it's sexy, it invites you in. Pink lipstick is a curse from the pit of hell.

I look up.

She tugs her bottom lip with her teeth. Classic move when you want to get kissed, but she's currently smiling into her cell, and she's not doing that for me, nor is she looking at me.

I snatch the whiskey bottle and dump more in my glass.

"Um," Dustin starts talking. "Do you think—"

"Not right now, Dustin!"

He holds up his hands. Are they shaking.? "Oh, um, okay well, we'll be there in the next forty minutes, so maybe, take it easy."

Bourbon splashes over my glass as I point to her with it. "Tell her that! She's half my size! At this rate we'll have to carry her."

Scarlett cups the phone with her hand. "Adrian says there will also be no carrying of me."

"He's not God!" I yell.

She nods. "Mmm, uh-huh, yeah okay, I'll tell him."

"He says you're a dum-dum." She grins and keeps talking. "Cool, I'll see you tomorrow. Love you."

Dustin gasps. "A love triangle!"

"There is no triangle! There isn't even a line! A square. A scratch on a piece of paper! No shapes exist," I clarify. "We're simply in the same car, sharing the same bourbon, and when we get to the winery we'll go our separate ways, right Scarlett?"

She puts her cell phone down then clinks her near empty glass with mine. "Right."

"Right." I just have to have the last word.

"Sure." She must know it.

Our eyes narrow at each other.

Dustin leans back and sighs. "It's like when the kids used to fight over the swings during recess when I was the recess monitor."

I crane my head toward him. "You were the kid with the orange vest and the clipboard, weren't you?"

He beams. "I was also a Cub Scout!"

Oh shit, he just saluted us; his chest could not be more puffed out.

I shake my head while Scarlett leans over and pats him on the knee. "The trauma you must have faced."

He frowns. "No, I mean, I resolved conflict."

"Sure you did, buddy." I nod. "Sure you did."

He yawns. "Wake me up when we're there."

He was out in minutes like a tired toddler, snoring and everything.

Scarlett sighs. "You totally beat up the hall monitors in middle school, didn't you?"

"No." I laugh. "I did steal their candy, though."

She gasps like I'm a murderer. "You stole candy from your fellow classmates?"

"I called it the candy tax." I smile as I nod. "And they paid up."

"Did you steal milk too?"

"How else do you down an entire Hershey bar?"

"Monster."

"Yeah, okay Prom Queen."

Her eyes widen. "Take it back!"

"Oh please, you scream popular. I bet you were prom queen, lost your V-card on prom night after the idiot that under-appreciated you put rose petals in a nice little trail toward the bed where he'd last three seconds then ask if it was good for you too while you sat there wondering what all the fuss was about."

Her mouth gapes, then snaps shut. She grabs the bourbon. "Maybe it's best if we just all take a time out before we arrive at Hell."

"Weird." I look around. "It feels oddly hot in here. I thought we were already at our destination?"

She rolls her eyes. "Silence, Leather Pants."

"Okay, Turtle Torturer."

We're quiet the rest of the ride.

I tell myself not to look at her every once in a while. Instead, like a lameass, I stare at her reflection in the window and wonder why I can't control myself around her, and why I walked away in the first place when all I wanted to do was run back.

Idiot.

And now she has him.

Brains are more dangerous than dicks. So yeah, I have reason to be concerned. Then again, most guys think with their dicks. What the hell do priests think with? Their hearts?

After setting my empty glass in the cupholder, I groan and lean back, closing my eyes. If she wants silence, I'll give her silence.

# TWELVE

## Scarlett

’m drunk. So wasted that everything is blurry in front of me, and any minute I’m pretty sure I’m going to puke all over the nice limo. Why is it spinning? Oh, yeah. I stare down at the empty bourbon bottle and giggle.

Oh, no!

I’ve got the giggles.

This is bad, really bad.

The winery is pretty from what I can see. Killian’s leaning against the door, eyes closed. Dustin’s awake and typing furiously on his phone, then brings it to his ear. “ETA one minute.”

Shit!

I quickly look at my reflection in my phone and grab some lip gloss, but it’s like I can’t find it in my purse. My eyes are bloodshot, my skin blotchy and swollen, and my hair’s sticking up like I slept.

Wait, did I sleep?

Or did I pass out?

I smile despite the fact that my stomach is rolling and my vision is so blurry, I'm afraid it's going to go full tunnel and I'm going to pass out the minute I breathe fresh air.

Pass out. I cover my mouth with another laugh. "She'd deserve it, that bitch."

Killian opens his eyes and stares at me. "The hell sort of language are you speaking?"

"I said she'd deserve it, that bitch," I clarify slowly.

Dustin leans forward. "Sweetheart, you said shesh deserva bish."

"Huh?" I frown. "No, I didn't. I may be drunksh, but I can… talk." I sway a bit and nod my head a few times.

Dustin elbows Killian. "Make her stop nodding, it's scaring me."

"You good?" Killian asks, leaning forward and peering at me with a narrowed gaze. "You look sloshed." He glances over at the empty bottle, and his eyes widen as though they might pop out of their sockets. "This was at least half full when I closed my eyes."

"And now!" I spread my arms wide. "It's inside!"

"Please, God, keep it there." Dustin swears under his breath. "All right, showtime. Killian, be on your best behavior. Everyone should be inside having a light afternoon lunch and happy hour, and since this one smells like happy hour, we should fit right in!"

"I could drink." I nod, then giggle. "I'm kidding."

"She's nodding again," Dustin whispers.

I sway forward and flip him off.

"Why did she give you a thumbs up?" Killian says under his breath.

"Maybe it means something different in her country of origin?"

Killian rolls his eyes. "She's Seattle born, idiot."

"Aw." I place my hands against my chest. "You member!"

Dustin makes a face. "I don't think you said what you think you said. Let's just not talk until we can get you all checked in and at your room, and oh, mother of God. Shit on me. Shit. Shit!" Dustin puts his phone away and grabs his leather bag, then forces a seriously scary smile onto his face. I can't tell if it's because I see three of him or if he's just… terrifying while I'm under influences.

Or the influence.

Influencer? Influencee?

I burst out laughing.

"Killian… I'm scared."

"Posh!" I yell, spreading my arms wide. "Isn't that what the Brits say?"

Killian shakes his head slowly. "Maybe my grandma."

"She still alive?"

"Shit on me. I agree with you, Dustin. All right, let's get the drunken one out of here and get to our rooms so we can rest before dinner."

He goes to open the door when it suddenly flies open and my dear, wonderful, hateful, mean little sister is the one that did it.

"Oh my gosh, you're finally here!" She pulls him in for a familiar hug while I reach for the bourbon bottle. A small goose egg on her head would be fine; her veil would cover the evidence and I'd feel vindicated.

Killian stands to his full height, and I clamber after him

in an effort to get out of the car and face her and not look like I'm ready to topple over.

Dustin swears behind me and gets out with that same creepy smile that makes me giggle.

"Oh." Addison's wearing a skintight white elegant strapless dress that goes to her knees and a pair of expensive camel-colored heels I'm sure they have a red bottom just like I'm sure she just got a light spray tan and Botox in her forehead with some filler in her chin. Her blonde hair is pulled back into a low bun with perfectly placed pieces of hair kissing her cheeks. Her gold necklace has a small diamond in the middle and the rock on her hand appears to need assistance being carried around or she's going to get tennis elbow.

Please let her get tennis elbow. "I'm confused. Why are you guys in the same car?" She fans her face and laughs. "What's that smell?"

"Sadness," Dustin blurts. "Arguing. And a bit of weird flirtation, but who am I to judge?" He laughs and rocks awkwardly back on his heels. "Um, anyway—"

"No, no, no." Addison takes a long sip of champagne, her eyes narrow on me. "There's no way you two are together. I mean, did you have car trouble?" She bursts out laughing. "Killian, you're the nicest rockstar ever, did you pick her up?"

She used his first name.

She's using him to play at her wedding.

She's a thief and a monster, and I want to pull her hair and watch every tiny little fake blonde piece burn up in flames then roast marshmallows.

God, I'm hungry.

My stomach growls.

"Hey!" I point a finger at her. Killian immediately grips my waist, so I don't fall face first into her. With my luck I'd knock her out and pass out snoring motor boating her boobs only to puke down them later.

Congratulations to the bride!

I laugh a bit at my own internal joke. Killian's grip tightens on me. "I'll have you know!" I wrap a firm arm around him and nearly die with how tight his body feels next to mine. Is he working out more?

I'm distracted for a few seconds before saying. "Ish totally possible! Oh, look." I point at the lobby. "Theresh shway!"

Dustin clears his throat. "I think she means this way."

"That's what I said." I lift my chin. Man, it's getting harder to concentrate. "And I'll have you know, we had shex—twice!" Why did I say twice? I can't even hold up a steady hand right now! "And it wasn't missionary!"

"Oh God," Killian whispers under his breath.

"It was against a wall!" I jab a finger in her direction. "And we did sixty nine—"

"There it is," Dustin says under his breath.

"And we LIKED ISH!"

"It. She means it." Dustin corrects me again.

"Is it a crime to shex your fiancé? Huh? Huh?" I mean, to say boyfriend, but fiancé just flows freely from my mouth.

Addison's eyes shoot straight up. "I'm sorry, fiancé?"

"YESH!" I shout. "We're going to have all the shex, get married and have beautiful babies together!"

Killian's grip tightens on my waist even harder, and he turns his head. "We should probably get you to your room."

"Oh!" Addison claps her hands. "I almost forgot, my

sister, silly one that she, um, is…" She literally looks me up and down twice before shaking her head and ignoring me again. "She didn't book her suite in time, and since she doesn't answer her phone didn't confirm her plus one for the weekend, so we put her in with Aunt Gertrude."

Horror washes over me.

Absolute horror.

I think I'm sober now.

Aunt Gertrude chooses that moment to sashay out of the lobby with two martinis, one for each hand, I mean, who wants lonely hands? Anyway, her short blue hair is impossible to miss. She's sturdy in her tall black heels and black dress that somehow manages to stay on her despite its every effort to fall from each ninety-year-old shoulder.

She stops in front of us and announces, "I just love olives."

And my day just got worse.

"But Aunt Gertrude, you're allergic. You know what they do to you." Addison laughs. "Then again, if you're really engaged, you can always stay with Killian."

She's challenging me.

She doubts me, as she should.

Tears threaten.

I hate her.

I hate this.

I hate that I'm too far gone for a really good comeback. And now I'm in the emotional state of being drunk.

None of this is fair.

Aunt Gertrude shoves one of her martini olives in her mouth. "See ya later. I'm gonna go see a man about a tryst in the vineyard."

Addison covers her mouth with a laugh. "Aren't you allergic to grapes too?"

"I'm old, we'll be fast, then I'll be back in my room, and he'll never know what could potentially hit him when I eat what I want." She winks at me. "See you later, sugar. Did you lose weight? You're positively gaunt and swaying into that strapping young man like your life depends on it."

I clench my teeth. "Oh, it just might."

Killian curses under his breath. "She's actually going to be staying with me. It's why this silly…" He squeezes my shoulder. Ouch. "…little pumpkinass forgot to book her own room, by herself, all alone." His grip tightens. "So, I'll just have my assistant…" He glares at Dustin. "…go check us in and if you could send someone for our bags too, Dustin?"

Dustin clears his throat. "Sure, sir, right away, I'll just—" The guy sprints toward the lobby doors like he can't wait to get out of this awkward situation.

Addison looks back at me, then down at my hands. "Where's the ring?"

Rob walks up awkwardly and puts his hand around Addison's shoulders. He's wearing a stupid black bowtie and a black suit like he's going to some event. Well, I guess it is his wedding, but it's still stupid.

His glossy hair is combed to the side, and I swear on all bourbon everywhere, the idiot has an identical fake tan to Addison's.

"The ring," I repeat, finally looking away from Rob. "It's um, the thing is…" Why won't my brain work?

Killian sighs and answers calmly, "She said she wanted one made of flowers wrapped around her finger to show the beauty, it's pressed in one of her favorite poetry books back at home, sitting next to Chuck Norris so he knows she's coming back soon. As far as a real ring, I thought we'd pick them out together, then get matching tattoos on our fingers."

God, and he was doing so good!

"Tattoos?" Addison bursts out laughing. "She can barely get a shot in her arm without passing out."

Tears fill my eyes. She's mocking me. It's over. Because who would ever believe that someone like him would end up with someone like me? I mean, even I couldn't believe it. He's so famous that other famous people fangirl over him.

"Well…" Killian locks eyes with her, then rests them on Rob. "When you have a partner you can trust, things don't look as scary." He leans down and presses a kiss to my forehead, then cups me by the cheeks, still basically holding me up.

His kiss is soft against my lips.

I want more. So much more.

I wrap my arms around his neck and press against him.

He groans when I slide my tongue into his mouth. Everything about the last horrifying moments disappears in that kiss.

This man's kisses taste different. They feel different, less like something you do because you should, more like something you do because you want to so badly that you can't help but take over and over again.

We break apart, breathless; his eyes flash.

If he started to strip me naked right now, despite all of our arguing on the way here, I'd help and be naked so fast his head would spin.

"Got the room keys!" Dustin announces, interrupting

our moment. "Let's get you guys… showered." He grins at Rob and Addison. "You know, plane ride, car ride… burritos."

Addison makes a face. "Burritos?"

"Don't ask." Dustin shakes his head. "They share a very personal and violent affinity for burritos. I think the gas station staff were preparing for a near brawl." He laughs.

Addison looks at me in confusion, her blue eyes reading way too much in my expression.

For some reason, I feel it's the best option to do a small bow, then grab Killian, turn around, and call over my shoulder. "See you at dinner!"

He helps me walk.

I feel like an idiot.

I gulp. "Thanks for the save."

He sighs heavily, then picks me up in his arms and carries me the rest of the way down the path. "Apparently that's my job in this anti-relationship."

"It was a nice kiss, though, even if you're hateful."

"It was a nice kiss, even if you're so drunk you probably won't remember that I saved you."

"I can't forget anything you do. Trust me. I've tried." I yawn, and the last thing I remember is him stopping, looking down at me like I'm not a failure, and me suddenly feeling sick and puking over his arm onto the exact path we're walking on.

# THIRTEEN

## Killian

I shouldn't have kissed her. I also shouldn't have picked her up because apparently it caused something to happen in her stomach, which means something happened near my shoes and narrowly grazed my right hand.

It takes a ten minute traumatic walk to get to our townhouse suite overlooking the Columbia River. It's modern, around three thousand square feet, and I'm actually glad that she's in my arms because she could easily fall off that cliff into the vineyards and go splat.

There are chairs for laying out, a bonfire pit, and a small hot tub out front, and when we walk in, everything is in blacks, whites, and purples. It's not too much, the floors are gray cement. And floor to ceiling windows give an incredible view of the cliffs below from the living room.

I walk into the master and gently set her on the bed, then go into the extravagant bathroom, grab a towel, wet it and walk over to her, wiping her mouth just in case.

She moans and flips onto her side. "Whyyyyyyy?"

"Because bourbon," I answer for her.

The front door opens. Dustin walks in with our bags and takes a look around. "Is she okay?"

"She died!" Scarlett announces.

I tilt my head. "I think, I think she's still drunk."

"I puked the drunk," she adds, a groan follows.

"Ah," Dustin sets down her black bag and garment bag near the closet and hangs up my garment bag. "Well, I'll make a coffee run then, the lobby makes incredible lattes. We'll sober her up before the dinner." He snaps his fingers. "You have the song ready, right?"

Everything in my body freezes. "The song? What song?"

Dustin's eyes widen. "The email? The request from the bride for a special song just for her?"

"NO!" Scarlett jolts up. "She doesn't get to have you sing to just her! That was my thing!"

She stumbles to her feet. "You…" She snaps her fingers at Dustin. "…grab me coffee, I'm going into the shower, I'm sobering up, I'm washing my hair and if anyone gets sung to it's me!"

She promptly turns and walks right into a wall.

"Oooh." Dustin makes a cringy face. "That sounded like cartilage."

Scarlett turns toward us. "I'm fine!"

Blood starts streaming from her nose.

What did I do to deserve this?

I walk over and pinch the bridge of her nose and tilt her forward and walk her into the bathroom, forcing her to sit on the toilet lid. "Stay."

Tears fill her eyes.

"And if you cry, I'm not helping you," I add. I'm weak for tears. I used to think they were pathetic, but with her? They make her prettier, and somehow, through the puking, she still has pink lipstick on. And it still makes me think of our kiss and how I wanted more, despite how much I want to strangle her for what she said.

If word gets out.

It won't.

It can't.

That's what Dustin's for.

I mean, this is a secluded private event, there are no paparazzi, and we said no pictures, the contract was extremely specific to avoid calamity.

Enter Scarlett.

She's a walking disaster.

Is it because of her ex or is it because of me?

I don't know. But I will ask because this is getting borderline ridiculous on both our parts. I can't seem to be fighting the girl that let me go. Neither of us wants to take the blame from eighth grade, so now I'm the one taking the blame for her supposed wedding night when I walked out.

I did the right thing. Right?

"I feel like shit." Scarlett sits on the toilet and hangs her head in her hands. Her hair's covering her face, but I know how pretty she still looks. "And I know I'm being ridiculous, but..." She takes a deep breath. "It just sucks, all of this sucks. I'm petty if I don't come to the wedding, right? I'm petty for not forgiving her or him, but—" She sniffles. "Did it have to be my sister? Did it have to be in our bed? Did it have..." She stops herself. "I need to shower and get ready."

She looks anything but ready.

And I'm truly afraid she's going to pass out in the shower or decide that a power nap under the hot water is the best idea she's ever had.

"Well…" I lean down and grab her hand. She jerks back at first, but I hold it firm. "The only choice you have is to march in there and pretend like none of it matters, get blindly drunk when you get home, and just power through the weekend. But first you need to clean up."

She looks over at the shower and sighs. "My Everest."

Even looking like a hot mess and she's still shockingly pretty. I release her hand, walk over to the shower, and start it. "You're not one of those girls, right?"

"Huh?" She frowns. "Use your words. I'm still half drunk."

"You know." I test the water. "The kind that freaks out over nakedness and can't handle a dick like an adult."

"I'll have you know, sir! I can handle dick like a professional!"

I burst out laughing.

She rolls her eyes. "Not like a prostitute professional or porn star, but like a normal healthy woman in her thirties who can handle dick, big, small, chubby, short, pencil shaped—whatever."

"Ah good, no prejudices. I like it." I cover my mouth with my hand to keep from laughing harder. "Then, we're both getting into the shower, you'll be happy to know you don't have to handle my dick, but I am going to help you wash your hair and get you ready."

Her eyes widen. "Naked?"

"Do you shower with clothes? Is that a thing?" I pull my shirt over my head and drop it to the floor. "Rules. No unnecessary touching, no pictures, and no thinking I'm hitting on you. This is specifically platonic, because if you show up looking like you just got run over by a truck, it reflects badly on your fiancé."

She rolls her eyes. "I was about to say I don't look that bad, but then I realized that would mean looking in the mirror and I don't want to scare myself. So, shower it is, just keep your parts to your parts."

"I can one hundred percent confirm all my parts will stay on one side of the shower." I reach for her tennis shoes and tug them off, followed by her socks. I tell myself that they're just shoes, that her skin is just skin. I completely ignore how smooth it feels beneath my hands when I tug down her jeans.

She lets out a little moan. "I might puke."

"At least wait until we're in the shower. Can you even stand?"

She gets up on wobbly feet. Her hips nearly smack me in the face. I stand and peel her shirt over her head.

She's not wearing a bra.

I ignore her perky breasts and make eye contact while tugging her black boy short underwear down to the floor. She's still leaning pretty heavily against me while I kick off my shoes and jeans.

Her eyes roam my body freely. Green eyes wide, she tilts her head. "You don't happen to have like peck implants, do you?"

I struggle not to laugh as she sways toward me, then pokes me in the chest with her pink fingernail.

I swat her hand away. "No, my boobs are real. Thanks for noticing."

She lets out another moan. "I hope this sobers me up."

"Says the girl who downed half a fifth of expensive whiskey. You owe me, by the way."

She scrunches up her nose and walks toward the shower; actually, she takes one step then falls back against me.

Her naked skin slaps against mine. I wrap my arms around her body and brace her tight. "Baby steps, let's get you into the shower. Think you can manage to lean against the wall?"

"Maybe." She yawns. "Yeah, I think so."

We walk into the rain shower and immediately it feels like heaven, I'm not even drunk and it's relaxing.

Scarlett moans. "This is better than sex."

"You've clearly been having sex with the priest."

"Ha-ha, very funny, and that was only like three times when we dated. He always felt too guilty."

I snort at that. "For sleeping with you?"

Idiot.

"No." She yawns. "For lasting too long. He was one of those marathoners that just keeps going and going and going—"

"I think I get the picture."

She reaches for the body wash and starts rubbing it down her body. "He used to do this one thing with his teeth where he'd graze a nipple and suck, then he'd grab a piece of cold ice." Her nipples get hard.

I grit my teeth and try to think about things that aren't sexy and that aren't nipples, like prison, murder, blood, clowns, Jenga.

Oh shit, the Jenga one was a bad call, because now I'm thinking about things going in slots.

I'd fuck her so hard against those blocks. The tower

would just collapse all over the place while I toss her against the game table and—

Scarlett taps me on the shoulder. "Your mouth's open and you just started panting. Is it too hot in here?"

It's hot everywhere.

I'm hot everywhere.

Self-control.

I grit my teeth. "Yeah, let's just hurry up, and no more talking about the priest, all right?"

"Aw, does it get you off?" She winks, cheeky brat. "Wouldn't be the first time I've been with a guy who was curious about Adrian."

I roll my eyes. "No, the priest doesn't turn me on."

She nods. "Then what's that?"

My dick is standing at attention in the salute to end all salutes.

I grab the body wash and start furiously rubbing it all over my body, then quickly rub it down her legs while she protests that I'm going too hard.

If I hear that word one more time…

I pull her under the water and run my hands up and down her slippery body and try to blank every space in my head. The shampoo smells like coconuts and a sweet, flowery perfume. I rub it in her hair and start to move my hands.

"Oh, God." Her eyes close as my hands get more aggressive. Her lips part.

I can't breathe. I've never washed a woman's hair, nor have I ever been so tortured in my entire life. Am I really that horny?

I quickly jerk her back under the water, blindingly add conditioner, rinse that out, then grab a towel and wrap her in it, furiously drying her off. I need to get the hell out of that bathroom.

"Whoa, kind of rough," she teases with a giggle. "I can't decide if I like it or hate it."

"Maybe a bit of both?" I say through gritted teeth, grabbing my own towel and wrapping it around my waist. I waste no time picking her up and walking her into the primary bedroom. I gently lay her on the white duvet and flip it over so she's covered. "I'll wake you up in an hour to get ready, all right?"

She yawns. "'Kay. What are you going to go do?"

"Finish drying off." I lie. "Sleep, and no more whiskey."

"Yes, sir." She salutes me. I take a few steps and she's already out on the bed with a smile on her face.

I exhale for the first time in the last ten minutes and jump back into the shower. I still need to wash my own hair, but my hands don't reach for the shampoo or conditioner.

They reach for the soap.

"Puppies, kittens, old grandmas—" I repeat over and over again. "Scarlett." I slip up and grip my length. Fuck, I'm so hard I can barely see straight. I grip myself tighter and tighter.

Nipples.

Soap.

Moans.

Shit.

I pump myself so hard it almost hurts. I rest a hand against the shower wall. I'm so screwed as I spurt all over the shower wall.

A knock sounds on the door. "You good, man?"

I stare at the wall, Dustin has to have heard that I went back into the bathroom. "Y-yeah, just... cleaning up."

"Cool, holler if you need anything."

"Yup."

I rest my forehead against the tile and bang it twice. "It's only a few days," I remind myself. "A few days, and I get women throwing themselves at me all the time. I can do anything for a few days."

Even if that means sleeping next to temptation herself.

# FOURTEEN

## Scarlett

It would have been the best nap of my life had I not had to suddenly use the bathroom. I could hear Killian back in the shower and figured I could probably sneak in or just beg him to look away.

How does a person go from failed wedding, to making out with a rockstar, dressing her turtle, puking in the rockstar's arms, announcing a fake engagement, and now peeing in front of him?

The world is a mysterious place.

Once Adrian gets here, things will be much better. He'll replace my drinks with water, he'll remind me not to lose my mind, and he's like zero temptation since he's off limits.

Whereas Killian…

Where do people get pecs like that anyway? You could bounce a quarter off them. I wonder if he could bench me.

No. No. Bad thoughts.

He has no interest in a relationship, abandoned me in my time of need, and on top of that, we apparently have middle school history.

We were doomed the minute I got those damn braces off, weren't we?

I slowly sneak toward the bathroom and crack open the door. The steam is billowing around his perfect ass.

I open my mouth to call out his name when I notice his jerky movements. Frowning, I peek my head farther in and gape.

Is he jacking off?

"Hey, man, you good?" Dustin calls from the other door.

I turn right into the wall, slamming the top of my left cheek against the wood before closing the door and sprinting back into bed.

Heart pounding, orbital bone breaking, I lay there for what feels like ten minutes before the bathroom door opens and Killian comes out.

I pretend to be sleeping.

Killian walks to the bed and stands over me. If I hadn't just seen him jacking off in the shower, I might be afraid he's going to reach for a pillow and shove it over my face.

Instead, I'm left wondering if the shower affected him as much as it did me. I mean, why else go back in there?

I can feel my body flushing from head to toe. I imagine my cheeks have a very naturally pink hue to them.

He was probably thinking about someone else. And it's perfectly normal for grown ass men to feel horny if they see boob; it could literally be the third tit of his aunt and he'd probably be horny.

Bad example.

Point is, boob is boob, and when tiny dick brain sees boob, they immediately want to touch, and then a light wind picks up through the house, and bam.

Boner city.

Ha! Yeah, that's it.

That's what happened.

There was a distant breeze brought on by the front door being open, it slithered under the bathroom door and announced itself to his dick and his dick's only obvious answer was to say hi.

Because that's what... dicks. Do.

I hear a rustling around the room and open up one eye.

"Agh!" Killian stumbles back. "Were you even sleeping?"

"Yes," I lie. "What are you doing? Why are you naked?"

"I have pants on, and I almost fell." His eyes narrow at me like he thinks I'm seriously unhinged, then he turns around and bends over to grab something out of his suitcase.

He's wearing a pair of ripped black jeans that hug his ass like he just got back from leg day and got too swollen. I gulp when he pulls a white V-neck cotton shirt over his ripped, tatted up body and follows it up with a leather jacket.

Of course he does.

And of course it's electric blue and somehow still looks devastating on him. His hair isn't even done, and I almost want to ask him to just keep that messy wet look, but that would mean speaking and I'm finding it hard to breathe at the moment.

Again, he wasn't thinking of me.

He was probably thinking of some supermodel or something.

He walks over to one of the tables and switches out one of his earrings in his right ear for a small dangly cross, then grabs a few rings from a box that must have magically appeared when we were showering. He follows that up with a matching cross necklace and grabs a pair of expensive looking sunglasses, I think they're Celine, but I can't tell and don't want to look creepy.

"So." He finally turns around. "You have around forty-five minutes to get ready. I'll go grab the coffee from Dustin, and you can get ready. Let me know if you need help picking out the dress that's supposed to murder the bride."

"Very funny." I crawl out of bed, forgetting I have the towel wrapped around me but not tied.

It falls past my knees. "Shit!"

"WHY!" he shouts and turns around in a circle. "Stop showing me your tits!"

"It's not on purpose!" I yell.

He looks back at me, his expression blank, and then a frown forms across his face. "What happened to your cheek?"

I touch the now swelling piece of flesh. "I uh, fell."

"You fell," he deadpans. "From what great distance did you fall while I was showering?"

"Bed." I gulp. "I mean, I had a dream you killed Chuck Norris—"

"The man or the turtle?"

"The man, and then I tried to punch the air and fell out of bed and hit my face on the side table."

"Wow, all within the span of like fifteen minutes and you were still able to get back to sleep? Impressive."

I laugh uncomfortably. "That's me, impressive. Besides, it doesn't look that bad, does it?"

I keep my towel tightly bound around myself and walk over to the mirror in the corner. "Oh shit."

He comes up behind me. "You could always say you got in a fight trying to save a little girl from getting trafficked."

I glare at him through the mirror. "A little dark for a wedding. Hey, aren't you supposed to be working on the special song for tonight?"

"I'm going to improvise." He crosses his arms. "You know, make shit up. Besides, we both know the only reason I'm here is to piss you off."

"The only reason you exist is to piss me off." I smile sweetly at him.

He leans down and rests his chin on my shoulder. I hate that I like the movement. What kind of cologne is he wearing? Or is that just hot rockstar musk with a side of tattoo? Asking for a friend.

Killian's chin is slightly rough against my skin; his five o'clock shadow should be illegal, he's clearly weaponizing it and knows it. "Why do I piss you off? Really, I want to know."

"Because." I lick my lips. "You're arrogant."

"You met me for a few hours and that's what you come up with? I'm arrogant?"

I'm annoyed with my own attitude. "It's not just—it's not just that. It's just… You know what? Never mind. I know we don't get along, and I annoy you, and that you're used to people just collapsing at your feet. Let's just get through the weekend and everything will be great!"

"Yeah, let's just hope my manager doesn't catch wind that I'm suddenly engaged to the girl that I was told in no uncertain terms to drop before my career tanks even further."

I freeze. "What?"

He shrugs. "You got the NDA, right?"

"Yes, the next day. Thanks for that. Basically, you'll sue

the shit out of me if I talk about you or share pictures of our moments together, super romantic. I literally got served papers, by a complete stranger, you know how humiliating it is to sign something that says no contact?"

"It says that?" he asks and scratches the back of his head, making his shirt rise up and giving me a perfect view of his low abs. "I just thought it was a simple, don't talk about Fight Club sort of thing."

"Uh, no, not simple, and I would never talk about you anyway like that, but whatever."

"How would I know?" He pulls away from me. I can't see his eyes because of his sunglasses, but I imagine they're piercing. "I only knew you for a few hours and while I don't make snap judgements, you were nothing but a stranger."

Nothing. I was nothing.

"Yeah, well now that we got that all cleared up." I move as far away from him as possible. "I'm going to get changed."

The room's chilly, the mood is anything but relaxed.

"Fine." It comes out snappy like we just got in a couple's fight, but you have to be a couple for that to be real and we're just like he said.

Strangers.

Nothing.

Absolutely nothing.

I take a deep breath and look toward my hanging garment bag. I have around six dresses to choose from. One of them is a form-fitting black number with a plunging neckline down the front and back, it creates a really cool V effect but shows a lot of boob.

I think of Killian.

And grab the dress.

# FIFTEEN

## Killian

"S o," Dustin says as he adjusts his black silk tie and tucks his black shirt into his black pants and grabs his black jacket. "How do I look?"

"Like you're going to an expensive funeral where they'll most likely have bottle service and Oscar styled gift bags, why?"

He shoves his black glasses up his nose. "I thought I looked professional."

"Or like you could be cast in John Wick Five, but sure." I pat him on the back. "Anything I need to know about for tonight other than the surprise song I'm being forced to sing for the bride?"

"Oh!" Dustin snaps his fingers directly in front of my face and grabs his iPad, ah, the scrolling again, what a treat. "Yes, so she saw this TikTok where this musician took different words about love and did a really cool compilation. Addison

called them her manifesting words. Kind of has a ring to it and—" He curses. "You're going to slap the iPad out of my hands, aren't you?"

"Was thinking about it."

Dustin takes a step back while I check my watch.

"I'm doing it on my terms. I'll glance at the words, but if she mentions anything about wheat grass, diamonds, or true love, I'm out."

Dustin hands me the iPad. "Well, I mean, she is getting married."

I stare down at the words and nearly choke. "Forever, Focus, Finally, Flourish, Fortunate, Forged, Faithful—" I pause. "Fluffy?"

"Apparently that's the new rescue cat they took in, kind of like her little kitten and—"

"Fuck me." I groan.

"Well, I think you could probably fit the F word in there since it does seem to be a theme, but there will be children present and… okay, I'm done talking now. I'll just let you stare at the screen a little bit longer—this is the new iPad, not the one you smashed last year, so just tread carefully. I'm only allotted one company device that's not my phone and I just downloaded—never mind, you don't care."

"Did it have to do with dinosaurs?"

His face lights up.

I shove the iPad against his chest. "Then no, I really don't care, and what the hell is taking Scarlett so long?"

I check my watch again. We've been waiting in the main restaurant lobby for what seems like ten years. Then again, I'm with Dustin. Time just seems to stop and not in a magical way where you want to spend the rest of your minutes in that moment, but in a way where you dream about root canals and that's your happy moment.

Dustin looks at his watch then glances up at the doors and does a double take, those damn glasses slip off his nose, he doesn't even shove them back up this time. Son of a bitch, someone will actually die today.

Scarlett walks through in what I can only describe as the most man-eating sexiest dress alive. Her heels are red, God bless her, and I see so much cleavage and curves that I can't remember how to use my hands or swallow, let alone give her a compliment.

Her hair's straightened down her back and her makeup is subtle yet gorgeous, with a light purple shadow and a nude lip. Is she wearing fake eyelashes or are those real?

She licks her lips and adjusts the small silver chain dangling between her breasts. "Sorry, forgot my purse and then I forgot earrings and then I had to pee, and why is Dustin pale?" She waves her hand in front of his face, then snaps her fingers. His glasses fall to the ground, he hurriedly grabs them and puts them back on and tilts his head.

Dinosaurs are clearly now completely extinct in any headspace he has available. All he sees is beauty.

Good thing he's all beast because, my date, my girl, not his.

I mean not mine.

Kind of mine.

For the weekend.

Damn it.

Dustin clears his throat and then bows like she's royalty. "You look perfect, Scarlett, wow who knew the girl who puked would clean up so…" Her eyebrows arch. "Well?"

"He was so close too." Scarlett looks at me.

I nod. "I was rooting for him that time, I swear it on my nana's grave."

"I thought she was alive."

"I mean, she could be dead."

"NANA DIED?" Dustin exclaims.

I take a deep breath. "Let's just go inside, have some fun, and try not to burn the building down."

Dustin gives me a weary look and narrows his eyes at Scarlett. "Limited amounts of alcohol, one glass of champagne to get you over the dog."

"Or in her case," I say, offering my arm, "shell of a turtle."

"Ha-ha." She takes my arm. "Been keeping that locked up inside until the right moment?"

"Nearly killed me," I admit. "But you have to say the timing was impeccable."

"I, for one, was moved." She grins, then stops walking with me. "Wait, hold on." She reaches up and tousles my hair a bit, her nails raking my skull like the orgasm of my dreams.

God, it may actually be better than sex.

Wait, what? I clear my throat. "What are you doing?"

"Nothing." She lifts a shoulder. Why is it so slim and creamy and what? Creamy? Just… beautiful and shit. I'm in over my head. "Just hanging out with my fiancé."

"Yup." Dustin agrees, like he's gaining points from looking so positive and happy. Fucker. "So in love, so in love, it hurts. Should we make our way to the rehearsal dinner? Yup, good call, always a good call, shrimp."

Scarlett immediately panics and stops walking. "Addison's allergic; there will be no shrimp."

Dustin laughs, then whispers under his breath, "I have Benadryl. Just focus on getting through the night and what happened with the song?"

"Soft kitty warm kitty little ball of fur," Scarlett starts singing under her breath.

I grab her by the elbow and look across the room full of people. "Not now, and I still haven't rehearsed. And I refuse to use all the F words."

She frowns up at me. "The F words?"

"Your sister only wanted words that started with F, they make no sense, and I refuse to die on that hill with my career on the line."

Scarlett tugs her lower lip. "What if you make it like... funny?"

"Huh?" I'm ready to pull my hair out. "How can I make that funny?"

"Just do like a parody? A comedy sketch with the song and call it good, like if she said fetish, you'd go into another word that rhymes, make fun of her in a good-humored way even though I want to strangle her, and then make it super short?"

I pause. "You think that would work?"

She nods. "Yup, and it's clever, it might go viral."

"Cool." I grab her hand. "Then you're doing it with me, fiancé."

"WHAT?"

"Bye, Dustin!" I wave and drag Scarlett in the opposite direction. "We have to make this epic and you're going to help. You ready?"

"No. Not in any way, no." Scarlett shakes her head then nods, "But also, I want to bring her down, so... yes?"

I hold up my hand for a high five. "See? I knew we could get along."

"Over a song for my sister?"

I wink. "I mean, I did sing for you."

"But that was romantic!" she points out.

I lean in and press a small kiss to her neck. "Yeah, it was. You ready?"

Her mouth opens and closes. "You're dangerous to my health."

I point at myself. "Sweetheart. I'm a rockstar."

She slaps me on the ass and whispers, "That's the problem."

# SIXTEEN

## Scarlett

'm completely sober and still ready to puke. My neck burns where he kissed me, and I can still feel the heat from his mouth right where my pulse is skyrocketing.

I'm still thinking about watching him and it's definitely not cooling me off in any way. I'm attached to him as much as I physically can be. Basically, I plan on being a growth on his person until this nightmare is over just so I don't get cornered by my sister, who is currently power walking toward me, golden hair pulled back in a loose ponytail and of course a white silk dress with a plunging neckline and—wait a second.

I stumble and look down.

I'm literally wearing the same dress in a different color.

What the hell?

I feel my cheeks heat; my jaw clenches.

Killian speaks through his teeth. "Question, does she

have spies or is this more of a normal, she set up random ring cameras in your house so that she can find out what you're wearing and try to one up you?"

I shake my head, and tears form in the most embarrassing way as my dad waves at me from his spot next to my mom. They're doting on her, smiling at her as if this is the best weekend of their lives. Not realizing that she's the devil. "Why does she always do this?"

I'm so confused and then I realize that last minute I sent my mom a few pictures of the dresses I picked out because I wanted to make sure they would be appropriate. My mom must have gotten excited about them and shown her. That means in under two days, my baby sister probably replaced her entire wardrobe in order to outshine anything I purchased.

I bite back a heated remark when Addison makes her way over and stops in front of us. A knowing smirk spreads across her face. If I didn't actually love her perfect pink lipstick, I'd punch her in the face, but the lipstick doesn't deserve violence.

No, that's just Addison.

I look behind her. "Lose the groom already?"

Her laugh is like nails on a chalkboard. "No, I'm pretty good at hanging onto my fiancé."

I dig my nails into Killian's arm. He lets out a cough and jumps next to me, then pats my arm. "Lucky for me, huh?"

I grin up at him. Nice save. If we were dating, that would def be BJ territory, but we aren't, for real. At all. So instead, I just smile up at him like he hung the moon and promised to buy me every star.

"Anyway…" Addison's gaze falls to Killian. She licks

her lips slowly like she wants him to notice and takes a step toward him that's dangerously close to being improper. "Are you ready for the song your manager promised?"

"About that." Killian puts one hand on his hip. "I was thinking of doing a duet. With your sister, since she loves singing so much."

Killing him later.

Addison bursts out laughing just as my ex walks up in his stupid tan suit and unbuttoned white shirt as if he actually has pecs to show off. Give him a long gold chain and he'd look like he was part of the mafia. "What's so funny?"

"Killian." Addison locks eyes with me. "He's going to have Scarlett sing with him."

It's his turn to chuckle after taking a sip of whiskey. "Scarlett can't sing. I think the last time I heard her sing it was when she was drunk and our dog joined in and started whining with her."

Yeah, and he's horrible at sex, but you don't see me shouting it across the rooftops, making a glitter sign or acknowledging that I was able to make a grocery list in the twenty seconds it took for him to finish.

Tears burn the backs of my eyes anyway. He left out the part that he had asked me to sing because he thought it was cute when I sang along to commercials and that Bruno would react every time.

I'm not sure if my entire body looks as hot as it feels right now, and I'm afraid to look at my own reflection. Rob may as well be sneering when he looks at how Killian has his arm around me.

"Baby..." He quickly looks away. "We should get back to our guests. Maybe it will give these two more time to practice, so Scarlett doesn't embarrass herself. I would hate that for her, and for you, on your special weekend."

"Good idea!" Addison winks. "I've heard the bathroom has good acoustics."

Killian wraps both arms around me and rests his chin on my head. "They do, we checked them out ourselves. Well, though I don't know if you want that kind of performance in front of your guests, things might get messy. I don't really have self-control with this one and"—he groans—"sweetheart, you can't just lean into me like that, I can feel your tight ass against my dick and I'm already struggling since the shower."

Addison's smile falls immediately.

Rob's eyes narrow as he looks between us with disgust, like shower sex is the epitome of the road to hell.

I turn in Killian's arms and mouth, "thank you," then wrap my arms around his neck and squeeze. "I can't help it, I like big things."

And damn, was he huge.

It's no secret that he really is actually swelling against me or that his eyes have this crazed look that even I would believe if I didn't know the truth.

"Wow." Addison's laugh is fake, flat, and loud. "Remember, we do have children here."

I look over my shoulder and meet her eyes. "Oh, that's right." Slowly, I turn to Rob. "We do have children here." His lips press into a firm line of even more disgust and anger. "I'm just gonna grab my date, cool him off with some water, and... practice."

We walk off toward the bar. I wait until we're next to the food before letting go of Killian. "I can't sing. I really can't sing, like I don't think you understand, I'm the worst."

"Good." He shrugs. "She deserves a bad performance, but, even if you're the worst singer in the world, how romantic would it be if we did a certain song together and then danced? Methinks it might steal her moment a bit, which also means you won't have to sing for long, and neither will I, and then we can go eat some shrimp cocktail."

I make a face. "I wish there *was* shrimp cocktail, she's allergic. She threw a fit when I had it at my reception and told me I was trying to murder her."

"Ah, at your own wedding, how very Dateline of you."

I smack him lightly on the chest and laugh. "I could get away with it."

He leans in and whispers low in his throat, "I believe you."

A shiver runs down my spine. I grab a bottle of water out of one of the many ice buckets around the bar and take a sip. "So, what are we singing?"

A drop of water slides down my chin, but before I can wipe the drip away, Killian's thumbs are already there. He smells so good and he's so close it's hard to focus on the beautiful balcony that overlooks the entire restaurant and lobby downstairs or the Vineyards just outside.

I break eye contact and take a step back, reminding myself that this isn't real, not even a little bit. "Um, so, what song are we doing? I'm guessing you're going to ignore all of the F words."

"Oh, there will be so many internal F words, but not the kind she wanted me to use when ordering me to make a special song. You know the new Taylor Swift?"

I roll my eyes. "I'd have to be dead, which one?"

"To all the girls you've loved before... but why don't we switch up one perfect word."

I gasp and smack him on the chest. "You're a genius!"

"Yes!" Dustin's voice sounds from behind us. "He really is, so I have the list of the words, and why are both of you looking at me like that?"

"We're changing the script." Killian grabs him by the shoulders and turns him toward the small stage. "I decided to do a Taylor Swift cover."

"We aren't licensed to—"

"It's a cover, I'm not stealing it, plus you'll love it."

"Should we maybe call management first and get this greenlit—"

"Oh shit, that reminds me, Dustin I forgot my throat spray back at the room. I can't do this without it, I'll freak out, you know how I get when my vocal cords aren't warm!"

Dustin actually salutes Killian like they're in the military and then runs off, yelling behind him, "You can count on me!"

When he's safely out the door, I turn to Killian. "Throat spray?"

"Meh, he's a slow runner when there are hills, we'll be half done singing by the time he gets back and by then he'll be so out of breath he'll be disoriented."

"You like torturing him."

"I think he actually likes the attention; you should see how his cousin treats him. The guy's certifiable." Killian grabs my hand and squeezes it. "All right, so I'm not going to give you a mic, I'm just going to have you sing it along with me like you're so in love you forgot it wasn't your own wedding rehearsal, all right? Make all the guests swoon; I'll do half the song, then congratulate the cheaters and we can go eat food. Sound good?"

"I like the food part the best." I scrunch up my nose. "But yes, it's good, I won't puke—again." Gross, I can still taste bourbon. Never again.

Killian slaps me on the ass. "Let's get out there and have a good game."

"Ouch." I rub my ass and stick out my tongue at his back and get annoyed when my sister watches us with narrowed eyes.

I know that look.

She still doesn't believe us. Which means I have to do this even if it's the most painful thing in the world. Killian grabs two black stools. I slide onto the first, trying not to give the guests a free show via the slit in my dress. Heart pounding, I wait for him to get adjusted on his own stool with the brown acoustic guitar.

Fender. Nice. He starts playing the Taylor Swift song. "When you think of all the late nights…" His voice is effortless, so effortless I almost forget to join in; I just want the free show.

He nods his head at me, plucking the strings of the guitar and locking eyes with me; eyes that say nobody else exists in the world. He gets to the chorus. "All the guys you've loved before."

I love that he changed it and that my ex is the one sitting by Addison and I get to sway and sing along with a rockstar… "But I love you more," he rasps.

I press a hand to his thigh.

It's just us.

Before I know it, the song ended, but Killian still has other ideas. He turns his head to the crowd. Everyone's clapping and smiling at us, and I wish again it was real. "Let's hear it for the happy couple in the back." His smile is wide, I know him well enough now to know it's all a show, it's his fake smile, I think I prefer his scowl.

I start to get off the stage with his help. I'm sweating in my heels and ready for the food that was promised to me, when Addison casually walks up to us and says through clenched teeth, "What the hell was that?"

Killian grabs a plate and starts piling it high with cheese, crackers, grapes, I follow suit. "A special song."

"You didn't use any of the words on the list." She seethes. "I'm paying you good money to be here."

"What can I say? I can't be tamed." He pops a grape in his mouth and smiles while I try to hold in the laughter. Her head is minutes from exploding. "Plus, I'm the artist, you're just the person who hired me, and in my contract it specifically states I needed to sing, so I sang. You're welcome. It's going to be all over the internet tonight, making you even more impossible to deal with."

I choke on my spit when trying to swallow and wait for her to strangle him or throw a heel at his face.

Her smile freezes on her face. "Stick to the track list for tomorrow."

"Yes ma'am."

She thrusts a polished nail right in my face. "And you!" I back up a bit and keep chewing. "Don't think I don't know what's going on between you guys. You've got everyone fooled, but there is no chance in hell you're actually dating." She snorts out a laugh and pulls out her phone. "Especially when he already has a girlfriend back in LA?"

Killian frowns. "Who?"

She shows us the phone screen. "Oh shit, I forgot about

her. I'm doing the song for her last movie, Shaylin James, I think? She's super sweet, she's also sixteen, so not only is that illegal, but I like a girl with an ass."

Me. I'm that girl.

Addison shakes her head. "Nope, I'm still not buying it." Her lethal stare refuses to let me blink. "Listen, I know you're jealous because I always get all the attention, but if you ruin my wedding like you ruined your own, I'll ruin your life."

"That was so many ruins," Killian says under his breath.

I almost laugh when her smile turns cold. "You weren't good for Rob, you sure as hell aren't good enough for a famous rockstar, and you've had spinach in your teeth the last five minutes." Her eyes rake over me one more time. "You even had to copy my dress. Unbelievable." She turns around and stomps off, head held high.

I wipe my face with the back of my hand, then jump toward her disappearing form, only to have strong arms come around me, pinning me in place. "Let me kill her."

"Violence solves nothing if you have so many witnesses," he whispers in my ear. "And your boobs are dangerously close to popping out of the top of your dress. The last thing we need is a nip slip."

I relax against him. "Fine, I won't chase her and force her to eat shrimp just so I can see her face puff up."

He slowly releases me. "As a fan of torturing horrible human beings, I'd probably just look in the other direction and at the very least drive the getaway car."

"Who's driving the getaway car?" A familiar voice sounds.

Panic slaps me across the face. "A-Adrian?" I smile. He doesn't know the story. He has no idea.

I thought his flight got delayed.

"Surprise!" He's dressed in a navy suit, with a white T-shirt underneath, and clearly just got a haircut. His messy dark hair is shaved high on the sides and longer on top. Honestly, he and Killian could be related. "Had I known my date was gonna look this smoking, I would have sprinted here." His eyes land on Killian. "Your services are no longer needed."

"Oh, I served." His eyes narrow as he protectively pulls me against his side. "And I'm officially her date, you know, since we're engaged and all."

Adrian's eyes bug out of his head. "You said yes to Mr. Illuminati over here?"

"Wow. Good one," Killian deadpans. "And I'm saving her ass and yours, a thank you is welcome anytime."

"I'm a man of the cloth, who shall not lie." Adrian reaches for his shoulder like he's going to pat it, then taps the leather jacket. "Vintage. Nice."

"Look." I step between them. "Let's not do this here. Let's just go back up to the room."

Adrian nods. "Lead the way. I'm assuming you already checked us in?"

Killian laughs and rubs his hand down his face. "I checked us in."

"No offense dude, but I'm not sleeping with you, not even with the voice of an angel." Adrian tries to grab my arm.

"Room." I grit my teeth. "Now."

My sister's already making a beeline in our direction.

"Shit!" I take a deep breath. "Act normal!" The guys share a look. "I mean, normal for you two! Just—don't argue, and if you can't lie, Adrian, don't speak at all. In fact, you are hereby muted until we get out of here."

He opens his mouth.

"Not a single word," I hiss.

He points to Killian.

"Yes, he can talk because he knows the entire backstory, and you're bound to over sell what you don't know, and somehow I'll end up pregnant with twins to trap this one into marriage, and you know what? Stop it, I don't like that look in your eyes." I glare at Killian. "Or yours."

"My eyes are normal."

"They're very green." I sniff.

"Thank you." He takes a step closer to me.

Adrian shoves an arm between us.

"So…" My sister stands in front of us. "I'm sure there's a story here somewhere. Or multiple stories." I can tell she's ready to sink her teeth into Adrian. She would be the type to sleep with him the night before her wedding. Thank God, Adrian knows how awful she is, not to mention he took vows.

"Actually," I pipe up. "We were just leaving."

She frowns. "You know, I did a head count several times and I could have sworn that on your invite you said plus one." She jabs a finger at me. "And the ex-boyfriend priest wanna-be didn't even respond, which leaves us at an odd number."

I can see the panic on Adrian's face.

"That's my fault." Killian sweeps right on in. "I'm the plus one and Adrian over here was embarrassed to go on his own, you know on the part of being bisexual and breaking up with his last lover, so we told him to come last minute so he could mend his broken heart." A groomsman walks by and releases a hearty belch. "What sheer luck you have, Adrian! Maybe he's free."

The guy in question is Rob's best man and so drunk he's currently swaying back and forth near the table.

My sister glares at him. "Mikey, if you can't handle your liquor, stop chugging it. I swear, if you puke anywhere near my dress tomorrow, I'll hang you by your toes from the nearest tree until you really blackout."

"Well!" Killian rubs his hands together. "On that scary note, I'll just take our half of the loverboyness, and go get freshened up again. He just got here, so he's exhausted."

Adrian nods.

"Between you and us, it happens when you're single and you just beat that meat so hard your hands start to shrivel up like other parts of your body. Exhaustion by dick is a real thing, especially when you struggle with becoming aroused, but…" He slaps Adrian on the back. "…lucky for us he turns himself on quite well! Don't you, little buddy?"

Adrian's nostrils flair.

"Anyway…" He turns Adrian toward the door. "We'll be back after the next threesome."

Dead. He's dead.

"Threesome?" My sister repeats so loudly that several people at the table next to us start whispering. "Not at my wedding. Gross, what? You lose one groom and now you sleep with anything? Even in front of your fiancé? You've changed, Scarlett. I'm worried for you."

No, she just wants to embarrass me.

"Um, don't knock it until you try it?" I offer in a weak voice while Killian escorts us out of the upstairs room and directly into Dustin.

"God provides again." Killian jokes. "Dustin, perfect timing."

Dustin tugs at his tie, sweat pours from his temples. "I looked everywhere, and then there was a—" He's making a motion with his hands that makes no sense. "Cat, giant cat."

"A giant house cat?" Killian asked.

"No, no," Dustin pants. "Chased me, there was so much screaming."

"I think he's hallucinating from the run." I touch his forehead. "He's clammy." We keep walking down the stairs, Dustin stumbles after us.

When we make it to the main lobby, Animal Control is outside and a small cougar's being put into a cage.

Killian bursts out laughing. "Oh, shit man, you got chased by a cougar? Please tell me you at least attempted to zigzag."

Dustin looks ready to puke.

Adrian walks around all of us and gives the cougar cage a wide berth when we make it outside and finally says, "A threesome? My male lover? What the hell!"

Dustin stops walking. "But there's four of us. What the hell did I miss while near death?"

Adrian hisses at the cougar. "Demonic ball of Satan."

I sigh. "He hates any and all cats."

"They have no soul," he mutters.

"Dogs do," Dustin says.

"That's because all dogs go to heaven, and who are you? I do like you. I mean, not enough to ever do you, not that *that* would ever be an option, but your theology is sound."

Dustin chirps right up. "Yes well, I did study world religions in college."

"Wow." Killian exhales. "It's already a really long evening."

I take a few deep breaths. "Let's just get back and strategize."

"Wait." Adrian stops walking. "Does this mean you really are staying in his room after I specifically told him to back off?"

Killian grins over at him. "We checked in and then I did what any respectful gentleman should do…" Oh no, oh no, don't say it, don't say it. I lunge for him, but I'm too late. "I got her wet."

# SEVENTEEN

*Killian*

**S**hould I have said it? No.

Should he have punched me? Absolutely.

Will my nose ever stop bleeding? Jury's still out on that one. "Seriously though, do I really need to wear a tampon in each nostril?"

"Yes," everyone says in unison after a wedding guest caught the entire thing on camera, so much for keeping a low profile. Dustin didn't help when he thought Scarlett's scream was the sound of the cougar coming back. He jumped onto Adrian's back while I crashed to the ground.

Dirt went everywhere, along with blood, as Dustin screamed, "Cougar!"

Which, I'm going to now assume they probably thought we were talking about Scarlett, not the actual cougar that was just roaming around the property after escaping his gate.

Scarlett's currently giving us all the silent treatment while

she changes, and when I joked about helping her unzip her dress, and truly meant I would help her, Adrian started throwing more tampons at my face.

Dustin went and sat in the far corner, a very distant look on his own face, most likely reliving dark cougar-like thoughts.

All in all, I think the trauma so far at the wedding matches the Jezebel getting married.

Scarlett finally makes her way back into the room. Adrian suddenly stands at attention like the sergeant just walked back in and he needs to pay his respects. Meanwhile, I'm still sitting there looking like either the best or worst tampon commercial in the world. Huh, maybe I'll endorse in the future.

"You…" Scarlett's in a matching white sweat outfit and has black Birkenstocks on. "…and you!"

Both me and Adrian get the finger point.

Adrian backs away slowly. "What did I do?"

"You exist!" She seethes.

I let out a low whistle.

"Oh, please." She grabs a pillow and throws it at my face, knocking one of the tampons out. Hey, I'm not bleeding anymore! "You don't just say things like that out loud! To people! Out loud! At a wedding! Out loud."

I raise my hand. "Are there going to be more out louds? I think I get the point."

She grabs another pillow and raises it high.

Adrian whispers next to me, "If you don't let her talk, she'll just get violent. One time I broke a toe, the memories too painful to recall, but know, it was because I spoke out of turn."

"Damn," I mutter.

Scarlett looks between us and throws the pillow to the ground. "Why are all good-looking men so stupid?"

Dustin clears his throat, finally joining the conversation. "I think it stems from their ability to get away with it."

"He would know," I say under my breath.

Adrian actually snorts out a laugh next to me. I mean, I'm kidding but I just can't help it, Dustin literally asks for it every time he opens his mouth.

Dustin points both fingers at me in an I'm watching you motion, then turns his smile to Scarlett. "I'll just go get you a nice glass of wine so you can relax."

She smiles back sweetly. "Thank you, Dustin."

"The pleasure's all mine."

"And mine," I say again, gah I just can't help it! What the hell is wrong with me?

Adrian groans next to me, then holds up his hands. "Yeah, I'm out, you're on your own. I do not need to get in the middle of this fight. Just nod your head and let her drink her wine. I'll be in the other room sending a prayer to Heaven for you."

"That's nice." I nod. "Thanks man."

"Oh, it won't help your dead soul, but it might just make me feel better that God's currently watching." He grins. "Good luck!"

Abandoned by both of them.

I pull out the other tampon from my nose, toss both in the trash, and sit back down on the bed. "I'm so—"

"—No." She shuts me down immediately. Damn it, she's pretty. "I don't want to hear that you're sorry I mean, I get that you're doing a lot for me right now but Adrian's my friend, Dustin's basically a stranger, well until now and my entire family now thinks I'm a wet whore currently shacking up with, two, no three men!"

"I mean..." I clear my throat. "Technically, we are all staying in the same suite so, you are shacking up in that you're living in the same space and your eyes just did something really scary, so I'm going to stop talking right now. Continue."

"Why?" She joins me on the bed and lays facedown. "You don't even like me, you just like pestering me so it's not even jealousy with Adrian, it's just that you can't help yourself."

She's wrong.

But I don't say it. Instead, I take a deep breath and move to the end of the bed. "Why don't you just rest for a bit before the final party tonight."

She groans into her hands. "I forgot about the moonlight wine tasting. Aghhhh!"

She starts punching the pillows around us, then sits up.

I pull back the covers and gently attempt to tuck her in, then join her on the other side.

"What in the hell do you think you're doing?" She tugs the blankets away from me.

I curse. "I'm going to rest too, I just got punched, Dustin was chased by a cougar, I performed a song, and at this rate, with all our arguing, I'm going to lose my voice before tomorrow's wedding."

She turns on her side; I'm almost afraid to see what she's going to say, but her cheeks are flushed, her lips are pale, and her eyelashes seem to be seducing me. "Poor baby rockstar with all his complaints, tell me you don't own at least three cars, two houses, can barely go anywhere without screaming and you're, you're…" She pretend chokes up like she's crying. "Worried about a wedding?"

My eyes narrow. "You're the devil."

"You have a Lambo, don't you?"

I immediately start getting itchy. Damn it, my skin! It's a rash! A rash! An emotional rash!

She reaches out her hand and taps my shoulder. "It's either yellow or green, something loud…" My face falls. "Oh sugar plum, is it green?"

"Just so you know, it is green and yes, I did accidentally tell a story about your pet turtle and how you dressed him up to go on a DATE with you to a WEDDING! And I'm not sorry!" I leave out that the woman had hearing aids and kept repeating, Urkel, which I'm lucky to even know considering I swear by the tv show Family Matters and the geeky dude who has two personalities, but whatever!

Scarlett lets out a gasp. "You told someone." Oh no, her voice just got deep. "That I made a tux… for my turtle. Out loud?"

"Am I the one that made you take that life journey? No."

"I hate you."

"I hate you too!" She tugs the blankets harder into her corner of the bed, nearly causing the small wall of pillows between us to collapse. "Out of all the stories you could have told, you told that one? THAT ONE?"

"I LIKE CHUCK!"

"WELL!" she yells back. "He hates you now, he just told me, we have telepathy."

"Oh God, here we go, what he can communicate with you through the magic ground beef you feed him? Don't tell me you left him in that tux, he could choke to death, it's like not cutting the plastic on the soda."

"Pop."

"Soda."

"AGHHH!" With one more tug she rips the blankets completely out of my hands, leaving me laying there in nothing but grey joggers staring up at the ceiling quite honestly wishing that Dustin would come in on a white horse and save me. How I ever thought Scarlett and I could get along, well, it's been a shitshow since day one.

Or I guess since lie number one.

"You started it." I find myself saying, and immediately regretting by the waves of anger I feel pulsing from her body at the moment.

She whips her head around and stares at me, it was a serious exorcist moment. "What. Did you just say?"

I gulp, then sit up on my elbows. "You're the one that said your boyfriend worked in the music industry and I'm the one that showed up with you by accident, might I add."

She sits completely up, the blankets drop, her hands are still in tiny fists and I'm pretty sure she's ready to punch me in the face. The only bonus is that her chest is heaving, and she's clearly not wearing a bra under her white tank top. It takes the power of a saint to keep me from looking for nipple. Instead, I zone in on her pretty brown eyes and wait for the attack.

"Listen." She seethes, her hair's all messy, pulled back in a bun on her head and her arms are braced for impact. "I meant like a producer or I don't know an assistant. I didn't mean the talent!"

I point at myself. "Talent. And it doesn't matter because

the minute they saw us together and everyone recognized us, they just assumed we'd been keeping our relationship under wraps for PR!"

"And Dustin!" She jabs a finger at me. "Nearly shit his pants so he just went with it, so really whose fault is this?"

"Gods," I say when she says, "Dustin's!"

I nod. "Not bad. I would like to use him as a scapegoat at some point this weekend."

"It's the mannerisms and all around fact checking for me." She looks away and nods like she's in deep thought. "Like earlier he asked if I knew how thick a turtle's shell was and I cracked a joke about—"

"—Teenage Mutant Ninja Turtles."

"Naturally." She nods. "And he was horrified, put a hand on my shoulder, then no joke patted me like I was in mourning and whispered in my ear, you know they aren't real, right?"

"Tell me you pretended to cry."

"Of course I did, because he felt like he was telling me Santa wasn't real. He offered me tissues and then his wine, which—"

"—You chugged immediately because, Dustin."

"Pretty much."

"He's a different one." I frown. "Hey, did we just stop fighting?"

"No. Maybe. Yes." She smiles. "You truly drive me crazy and not in a good way; you argue over the dumbest things."

I hold my hand up to stop her. "No, I just like to have my opinion heard."

"Ergo, arguing," she responds.

"Which is what you're doing right now."

"Must you always have the last word?"

"Must you look so pretty with no makeup on and your hair looking like a rat nested in it?"

She opens her mouth and closes it, then crosses her arms over her chest. "Low blow."

I chuckle and get a pillow immediately to the face. "Ouch."

"Deserved."

"Fair."

I sigh and then flip over to my side. She's right there, so close I can taste her. Brown eyes lock on mine. I lean down, knowing that everything in me is saying this will end badly, but I just want to kiss her. I don't know if it's because she never gives in, or because she looks so cute with her hair and makeup free face, or if I'm just going crazy from this wedding.

But I want it.

I slowly lean down while she leans up on her elbows. I'm a breath away from her mouth when Dustin's voice rings clear.

"AUNT GERTRUDE IS DEAD!"

We break apart instantly; he knocks on the door then bursts through it panting. "Aunt Gertrude! She left her teeth on the table, she got drunk, they can't find her, they think possible drowning in the pool, the pond, the SEA, I mean, river, whatever, we have to find Aunt Gertrude!"

I hold up my hand. "Not that I'm not panicking like you are right now, but why is Aunt Gertrude so important?"

Scarlett freezes next to me. "She may be weird, but she literally has control over the entire family money. I mean, if I sneezed funny while she farted after eating one of her ten allergic foods, she'd say I was out of the will."

I roll my eyes. "Okay, so what? Are we talking like two million? Five? Ten?"

"Seventy." Scarlett and Dustin say at the same time while Adrian comes running in.

"Aunt Gertrude is missing!"

"We know," we say in unison.

"She's worth seventy million and changes her inheritance like people change leases!"

"We know," we say again in unison.

I take a deep breath. "Okay, let's split up and also acknowledge we're doing this to save a life, possibly a shitty wedding, and it has nothing to do with money."

Everyone goes silent.

"Welll…" Dustin holds up his finger and thumb.

Adrian sighs. "It has a little to do with the money and it not going to Addison because last year she was cut out."

Everyone freezes.

Scarlett goes pale. "I'm sorry, what?"

Adrian looks down at his feet. "Your dad made me swear."

She smacks him with a pillow. I really need to start hiding those. "WHY!"

"Because!" Adrian starts to pace. "He knew it would upset you because it's your sister, but Gertrude was pissed over what Addison did and said. The only way she'd forgive her would be to settle down and stop her whorish ways, and she did say whore."

Scarlett isn't really moving. I wave a hand in front of her face. "You with us? You breathing?"

"What did I ever do to her?" Scarlett whispers, her voice is too soft; it's freaking me out a bit. "I just wanted to be happy. I wanted her to be happy—"

"—she wants money, she has no job, her hobby barely pays her because nobody cares. What do you think?" Adrian sniffs. "You have a successful podcast, so she of course, tries to start one. Everything she does is a carbon copy of your life, so worst-case scenario if she can't be you—"

"—She'll beat you," I say under my breath.

Dustin lets out a gasp. "It's like Dynasty."

"How is this like Dynasty?" I ask.

"Nevermind." He waves me off. "Let's focus on the missing aunt first. Cops have been called, security is out looking, even Killian's bodyguards, but we should at least attempt to help. Anyone know where she would most likely go while drunk?" The room goes silent for a few seconds, then Scarlett jumps up. "She loves swimming."

"Well, that does not bode well for us," Adrian says under his breath before, "Father, forgive me, I have sinned."

I roll my eyes. "Let's go, they have at least five ponds on property, two pools, and a giant ass river called The Gorge, fingers crossed she didn't venture to the four-thousand-foot-deep section where people go to an eternal sleep."

"Hey!" Dustin holds up his hand for a high five. "You have random, useless information too, up top."

"Do not." Scarlett shakes her head. "Hit his hand."

"Do it man, do it for me." Adrian nudges me in the arm.

I lower my hand. "Whatever. Let's go find the missing aunt. I'm sure she's fine."

Scarlett doesn't look convinced, and I know I'm probably not helping with my grumpy demeanor. She runs off in the other direction and creepy as it may sound, I wait a few minutes than follow.

Something about her alone in the dark doesn't sit well

with me. I mean, I know she's strong and can handle herself and we're not technically in a real relationship, though we argue like we've been married over a decade.

A smile forms across my lips before I can stop it.

Why am I so pulled to her? And why do I want to equally shove her away? She deserves more than life on the road, that's for sure. On top of that, I'll break her heart.

It's what I do.

I freak out; I don't commit the way I should. I panic and think about myself and my career and then I just bounce.

She deserves the priest.

But it will be a dark day in hell before that happens, even if it's me falling on my own sword.

Which just makes it worse. I can't have her, but nobody can?

"Shit." Gravel crunches under my shoes as I follow her into the darkness, and I can't help but wonder why it feels like it's light.

Maybe it's her.

# EIGHTEEN

## Scarlett

'm too stressed out and confused to do anything but just run in one direction while the others run opposite of me. I know of one pond close to us that's near the lobby, but I can't imagine Aunt Gertrude just throwing caution to the wind and jumping in.

For one thing, it's super dark out despite the different path lamps they have at the resort, and for another, she usually takes a… um, lover with her and when I consider the way that would even go with water, I want to vomit bourbon again.

How did Adrian keep that from me, though? The fact that she kicked Addison out of the will? Is that why she's getting married or am I just jumping to conclusions? It's not like Rob doesn't have loads of money.

Unless they're broke.

No. That would be crazy. His family is literally a dynasty of Seattle, though he did ask my dad for significant investments into one of their new projects.

See? Now I'm going all detective on something that isn't even an issue because I'm stressed out and I hate being lied to.

Damn it, Adrian!

Why couldn't he have just told me? Is it the whole priest secrecy thing? Protecting me? He knows I don't even care about the money, and while Aunt Gertrude is eccentric, I love her, she always has the best jokes, and she throws back tequila like it's water.

What's not to love?

In my Birkenstocks and white sweats, I trudge over to the nearest pond that I'm sure everyone has already looked in and turn on the flashlight on my phone.

No movement.

Huh, don't they at least have fish in there?

"What the hell are you doing?" Addison's voice is truly like nails on a chalkboard at this point and I'm way past being annoyed, even if it *is* her weekend.

I lower my phone and look over my shoulder. She's dressed impeccably in this weird tuxedo looking pantsuit that has her breasts on full display down the middle with a little matching black choker.

Ha! What if I just choked—her?

I smile widely at my own joke. "I'm helping the search party."

Addison waves me off like nothing matters. "Whatever. She took out her teeth then crawled under the table, but the tablecloths were too long so nobody thought to even look, and you know how short she is, anyway. If one more person ruins this wedding, I'm going to go psycho bitch on everyone."

Bite your tongue. Bite your tongue. Oh, the good Lord (if he's real) will bless me for this one, he shall bless me with thousands of free dollars at Nordstrom, a yacht, ten men. Zac Efron, Austin Butler, Jungkook, Keanu Reeves, Yunxi Luo, Dylan Wang, Channing Tatum, Timothee Chalamet, John Boyega, and Tom Hardy.

Amen.

I take another deep breath, so I don't end up on one of those crime shows and force a smile. "I'm so sorry this has been rough for you."

That's all I have.

It's truly all I can give to both her and the cursed universe.

"Rough?" she repeats, her eyes venomous. "Rough?" Her hands turn into tiny fists, ready to pummel me. "Did you know that they tried to bring in shrimp? SHRIMP!" She clearly needed to yell it twice. "Someone's obviously trying to murder me."

Yes, obviously. For what reasons? Oh, weird, no clue. Stares hard at exhibit A.

"And then!" she continues, "Rob just leaves for a few hours to go play poker and comes back smelling like skank? I swear if you slept with him, I'll—" She heaves and stomps on the ground, getting tiny dust particles on her cute jumpsuit. which I find oddly satisfying. "Kill you! He's mine. He's always been mine. He's from money. He knows what he wants, and you were just this little attraction he couldn't get rid of. You've always been like that with every boyfriend. Oh Scarlett, she's so fun, she's so chill, and then boom, they meet me and realize what's real."

Tears start streaming down my face. Is she wrong? No. I was the fun one, she was the hot one. I was the one with the personality. She was the one with perfect skin and nails and clothes. Which begs the question: why copy me?

"Anyway." She sniffs. "I guess it doesn't matter. I'm the new family favorite. Gertrude adores me. We're going to Maui next May."

I sigh. "Good for you."

"And," Addison adds as she puts her hands on her hips like she needs to look more in control or demanding, "I have the perfect man. So who officially wins after all this torment? Me. I win."

I would literally win if I had a shower and another glass of wine. "Addison, what did this? What separated us? I truly want to know. Back in high school we were still close and then—"

"He used me," Addison whispers, "to get to you. He said if he could get close to me, he'd get close to you."

"Jason?" I ask, showing my disbelief. "Because he literally only comes out of his parents' basement for cold pizza, then goes back to the sad dark little basement and plays Xbox with ten-year-olds."

"I liked him, and you don't deserve her money!"

"Okay?"

"Don't you get it, you take everything from me!" She stomps her foot in the way you'd normally see in movies, but right now all I see is dust swirling around me and then a hard push into something cold, ominous.

Oh yay, I'm going to drown.

I swim up to the surface, realizing that my own sibling just tried to murder me, and attempt to get to the side only to hear a splash to my left, and feel warm arms surround me. "Don't die, you annoying little minnow."

"Worst romantic phrase ever." I choke out so much water that my throat burns. "But thanks for bringing me to shore, Aquaman."

Killian laughs and pulls us onto the cold, hard, dirt-filled ground. "Well, I do try."

I let out rough exhale. "Is she after love or money or just hatred for me?"

"Maybe all of the above?" he offers. "I learned a long time ago not to actually try to figure people out, because, for the most part, you'll deal with a painfully wrong scenario. You just accept things at face value, value them the way they value you, build them up, and hope that they'll be the vision of the person you saw in the first place."

I can't help it. A tear runs down my cheek, hot, aching, needy for someone to say it's okay. "Why do you have to be so romantic when I want to punch you?"

Strong arms pull me tighter until I'm pressed against his body. "Maybe because you're growing on me, and I kind of want to water the plant more, see how it sprouts, cut off a bit of flower, use my fingers to—"

"You always have to make it dirty."

"I was literally going to say move around the soil so more could sprout up and here you are reprimanding me. Man, I can't even win with you so—"

"I like you," I blurt. "I mean, I'm just sitting here on the side of the pond with my thoughts and emotional demons and all."

"I think I have a song that starts like that," he muses.

"Bet it's awesome."

"Double platinum. Thanks for the validation." He laughs before grabbing my hand. "Holy shit, are you okay?"

It's almost like his words registered the pain in my palms

as I sit up. I have several goat head prickers stuck in my skin, feeling like the fires of hell. Not a big deal, no infection, but still not fun and getting less fun by the minute.

"Hold on." He jumps to his feet and gently grabs my elbows and pulls me up. Immediately, he starts pulling out the goat heads and tossing them to the side.

"There's a lot." I squeeze my eyes shut. "I hate things being stuck in me!"

Killian bursts out laughing. "I hope not all things."

"Oh, ha-ha, very funny, manwhore."

"Don't knock me until you try me."

I freeze and open one eye. "I don't know if I could handle you."

"Funny, I was thinking the same thing about you," he whispers. "All done." His eyes flash before he leans down and blows on my palms.

I think part of me is dying inside, at least that's what I'm feeling as the cool air tickles my skin.

His lips are perfect.

He looks up. "What?"

I shake my head, unable to form words.

"Nope, you just had the most curious look on your face I've ever seen."

My face is hot. I'm blushing. I have to be blushing. "I uh, just was remembering something."

"Your name?"

I roll my eyes. "No, the way you taste."

He freezes, then slides his hands up my arms. "Did you want me to remind you?"

Slowly, I nod my head. "Might be a mistake though, crossing some lines, jumping over barriers."

He grips the sides of my head. "Fuck barriers."

Our mouths are colliding before I have time to think, his tongue is soft against my lower lip before sliding into my mouth and I swear I taste him everywhere.

I cling to him like my life depends on it.

His hands dive into my hair while pulling me closer and closer until our bodies are slammed together the way our mouths are. He's delicious, soft and hard at the same time.

It's like he went to a special rockstar school where they taught every hot musician how to properly kiss and hold a person with just the right amount of pressure. Damn.

He breaks away first, his eyes lost in mine. "Remember?"

I start to shake my head, no. His eyes crinkle at the sides as he smiles and leans down again, only to, of course, be interrupted by shouting.

"RUN!" Dustin's voice sounds. "It escaped THRICE!"

"Is thrice even a word?" Killian asks out loud, still not letting go of me. "Because it kind of rhymes with mice and wait, why is he running toward us?"

"GO!" Dustin screams. "It's out!"

He's not wearing a shirt.

He has no shoes on and there are goat heads, not to mention whatever sharp rocks he can trip on. "Huh," I wonder. "He's really freaked out."

Dustin keeps running. Sure enough, right behind him is what looks like a large tom cat with what I'm assuming is Dustin's shirt over its head.

"Should you tell him or should I?" Killian asks.

I cross my arms. "Honestly, I think I'm enjoying this moment the most. Maybe we just wait for him to catch his breath?"

Killian nods. "He's gonna tucker out, eventually. Oh, look! He zigzagged." He starts clapping, then calls out. "Good job, little buddy!"

Dustin runs behind us and pants. "Get it, get it!"

"Hey, there." Killian leans down and grabs the shirt off the cat. "Did that big dummy scare you?"

"Oh, I'm sorry. I was busy getting chased by a large feline! TWICE! THRICE!" He starts to whimper.

"Bro, you were chased earlier for like two minutes, and this isn't even a cougar. It's a stray cat. You have cat issues, I'm concerned." Killian pats him on the head.

"No!" Dustin jerks away. "Did you know cougars can travel up to fifty miles an hour? Sometimes are accused of eating their young? THEIR OWN OFFSPRING, just like mountain lions, which fun fact—"

"Someone needs to take away your ability to search random facts on the internet," I chime in. "Because, wow."

"Oh, please." Killian jumps right into the conversation. "You literally Googled if you were going to die because you saw one Oprah episode where someone was cutting celery and ended up needing her arm amputated. You still can't cut with real knives!"

"Shots fired," Dustin says under his breath.

"I told you that in secrecy because we were sharing, and I was having a rough moment when you rescued me from the cheating bastard screwing my sister!"

"But does he do it well? Does he"—Killian smirks— "stick it well?"

"Why did I even kiss you again?" I wonder out loud.

Dustin stills. "You guys kissed?"

"She nearly drowned," Killian says helpfully.

"There were goat heads," I add. "It was romantic."

"Errr, yeah." Dustin looks between us. "That sounds super romantic, from near death to pain to this... yup, should probably light a candle, sing some Celine Dion."

"Hey!" we both yell in unison.

"She's a national treasure!" Killian adds.

I offer up a high five.

"Hmm, more terrifying..." Dustin stares at one hand. "Cougars, or you guys arguing, then getting along because of Celine Dion. Decisions, decisions."

"Hey!" I look around. "Where's Adrian?"

Dustin pales and looks down at the ground, then at his hands. Why the hell are they shaking? "So, he, um, discovered Gertrude."

"Good for him." Killian offers up his hand for a high five.

Dustin does not hit it. "Yeah, man, I don't think he's going to look at it that way. She was so wasted when he found her under the table that she just dragged him beneath it." His voice lowers to a whisper, "She's so strong."

I frown. "Wait, she just pulled him under the table? Because she needed assistance?"

Dustin shrugs. "I mean, nobody is really sure what happened, but there was some moaning, a few cries for help, and then when we finally got to him, he just stared at us with this long blank stare. But Gertrude found her second wind, grabbed those dentures, and then went back on the dance floor. I'm sure everything's fine though. He was heard saying the Lord's Prayer. Normal for a priest, right?"

Me and Killian share a look; he shakes his head. "He's gonna need us."

"Solidarity. If there was communion wine, he'd be neck

deep in it. Gertrude is the best, but when she's on the devil's liquor…"

Killian nods. "Let's go check in on him."

"Oh!" Dustin claps his hands together. "He's back at the room getting ready since we have that moonlight tasting and food tasting and why are they planning things so late in the evening? I just want to sleep."

Killian presses a hand against his face and yawns. "I'm the worst rockstar ever. A nap sounds lovely."

I giggle. "You said lovely in the most British accent ever."

He turns and winks at me. "But did you like it?"

I swear every part of my body spins out of control, between chills, goosebumps, and insane attraction, I freeze. I can't even look away. I'm expecting him to joke again, but instead he reaches for me, gripping the back of my neck.

I gasp. His smile is so beautiful it should be illegal and tragic all at once because how does a person ever move on from that sort of smile, with dimples on each side, a strong jaw, just the perfect amount of a five o'clock shadow, honeyed dark hair and glory?

"I'm gonna kiss you now." He looks over my head. "Dustin, cover your eyes."

"What? Why?"

"Fine," I whisper. "I'll just cover mine and imagine an insanely good-looking rockstar decided to seduce me."

"I can hear you!" Dustin yells. "God, you haven't even signed the papers!"

"Papers," Killian repeats. "Burn them all."

"Why are you both so charming and so argumentative? I can't decide." I sigh and lean up on my tip toes, meeting his soft lips.

He presses an eager kiss to my mouth and pulls away. "Because it confuses you enough to stay."

"Was I leaving?"

His expression darkens. "It feels like everyone does."

"Oh, look! A duck. Swimming on by. With an oar!" Dustin exclaims loudly. "No need to talk about family history out here. Remember, Adrian just got seduced by your aunt! Ha-ha!"

"What if I don't?" I ask. "I mean, you're kind of stuck with me for now."

He grins. "I don't have a choice."

"You never did."

I'm so far gone when his mouth meets mine again that had I not been in pain or aware of Dustin watching us I probably would have stripped Killian fully naked and had my way with him even though I'm fully aware it's a horrible idea. I have no business wanting him.

He has no business kissing me.

And yet we can't stop.

He lifts me into the air, his hands on my ass, pressed fully against my front, mouth latched onto mine. God, he tastes good.

Dustin clears his throat. "Ahem, we should probably go rescue Adrian and do our duties as guests."

"Duties," Killian says against my mouth, rubbing himself against me. "Never sounded so good."

"So good," I repeat. "So hard."

"Yes." Dustin coughs. "Duties are very difficult, and I am still here. I exist."

"Good for you," Killian yells. "Give us five minutes."

"Oh, look a child born out of wedlock, just over there," Dustin yells. "Seriously, you both need to come."

"Yes." I grab Killian's shirt and tug him closer. "We do."

"So bad," he agrees. "What the hell have you done to me, you heathen?"

"Need," I moan.

"WHY!" a voice sounds.

We break apart. I slowly, achingly, slide down the front of Killian, feeling every inch of glory and turn. Adrian's standing there, mouth swollen, eyes wide.

"You good?" I ask.

He shakes his head slowly. "Forgive me, Father, I'm about to sin."

"Oh, shit," Killian whispers under his breath. "He looks like he saw a ghost."

"Demon," Adrian corrects. "With lipstick."

"Did you at least have fun burning in hell?" Killian jokes before Adrian makes a lunge toward him.

And that's when I bolt.

I run, laughter bubbling out of me.

Killian follows, gripping my hand.

Dustin's cursing.

Adrian's even cursing and stumbling. I can't one hundred percent decipher what he's saying, but I'm pretty sure he's quoting Dante's Inferno—by heart.

We make it across the road and back to the suite before he can get us, but resistance is futile. The minute we get inside, Adrian yanks open the door. "She asked me to suck her—"

"Nope!" I cover my ears. "Nope, no sad words!"

"Pearls," Adrian finishes. "And I think she meant something else."

Dustin exhales a long breath, then pants a few more times. "There, there, I'm sure she meant pearls."

"There was no necklace present," Adrian admits, running his hands through his damp hair. "I don't want to go tonight."

"You're our date." Killian grins. "You have no choice. Just run in the opposite direction if she makes eye contact."

"Easy for you to say. You weren't asked such… unbiblical questions!"

Killian rolls his eyes. "You're a grown ass man. Just say no."

He whispers, "She's very strong."

"Hey!" Dustin yells. "That's what I said!"

"This is not a time to celebrate her strength," Adrian whispers. "Let's just get through the wine tasting, and not die. Amen."

Killian makes a cross with his hand while Dustin nods solemnly. You'd think we were going to a funeral. Then again, it is Addison, so who knows what fresh hell could be unleashed.

I take a deep breath. "What's the worst that could happen?"

"Pearls," all the guys say in unison, and I have to say…

They have a point.

# NINETEEN

## *Killian*

**S**hould I be kissing her while getting random texts from my agent, asking how the hell I'm already all over the internet singing Taylor Swift to a woman who's not the bride?

Angry Agent
Tell me I read that breaking article wrong. Tell me you aren't serenading the girl from last time and tell me it's not true you're engaged.

I sigh and stare down at my phone, then back up at Scarlett. She's in a gorgeous black dress, mourning, according to her, the loss of my mouth, which just made me want to kiss her harder. She takes a long sip of wine.

Shit, I'm in trouble. I won't want to walk away again.

How has it only been one day? A very long day, but still. Scarlett's pink lips meet her glass again. Adrian stares me down and shakes his head slowly, it's like he raided my

closet with his ripped tight jeans, brown boots and tight gray YoungLA shirt that basically every bro at the gym bro-ing wears like a religion. Somehow, they figured out how to get the perfect cut on the biceps, which means you look jacked even if you aren't.

I glare. Too bad Adrian actually is jacked. He keeps looking over his shoulder, and I may keep widening my eyes, pretending to silently warn him, *"Gertrude's behind you."* He's not amused.

I quickly type back to my agent.

> Me
> Don't worry about her, it's just a little... acting this week. Once I get back, I'll make sure to squish the rumors and I'll be more careful. It's nothing.

> Angry Agent:
> It better be nothing, you know what happened last time. Getting entangled with crazy fans isn't the best look and to be with her again at her sister's wedding. I thought she wasn't even going? This was supposed to help you look like the hero, not like the guy that's still obsessed with the bride he stole a year ago.

I groan into my hands.

> Me
> I'll take care of it.

> Angry Agent
> This is on you if it blows up and then it's on me. Tell Dustin to do his damn job!

I toss my phone onto the table.

"Trouble?" Adrian asks, reaching for another one of the appetizers in the middle of the table for the wine pairings.

I shrug. "Nah, my agent just has something up her ass."

"Always has something up her ass," Dustin grumbles.

"I'm going to go get more of that dish with the sauce."

"Descriptive." I nod.

"The pasta thing?" Adrian jumps to his feet. "Get me some too?"

"Sure." Dustin stands and starts to move away when Adrian jumps to his feet, eyes wide. "Actually, I'll go with you, good sir! Ha-ha!"

I frown. "You need to work on your fake laugh."

"It's because I'm pure." He rolls his eyes, then shoves Dustin in front of him just as Gertrude makes a beeline for our table.

I smirk over at them.

"What?" Scarlett moves seats and pulls the chair out next to me. "Adrian's purity?"

"Yeah, I mean, he said that with a straight face while using Dustin as a human shield."

She clinks her glass with mine. "I think Dustin is too focused on the buffet table to notice that Adrian's using him improperly."

"Hmm." I glance back at Scarlett. "I like your lips."

She chokes on her glass of wine. "Thank you?"

I tilt her chin toward me with my thumb and forefinger. "Are we going to be alone tonight, or do you think we'll have to babysit?"

"You're rich, right?" She leans in and presses her hands onto my thighs. I don't even pretend to hide the fact that I'm already aroused. "Maybe you just pay them off. Adrian's going to be watching you like a hawk, and Dustin won't stop shouting about papers."

Which reminds me.

I cringe down at my phone, then slowly shove it into

my tight jean pocket. "Yeah, well, sometimes things happen, and the team always wants me covered."

Scarlett nods and stares down at her lap. "So, what's next for you after the reception?"

I lean in. "I could take a few days off."

"Where would you go?"

I shouldn't risk this, I shouldn't waste my time because when she does find out, which she eventually will, it's going to be game over and I'm going to be wrecked.

I know I'm already invested. I was invested a year ago, but how does a person even bring up that conversation?

"Mom." Scarlett moves to her feet. "You look great!" Her mom doesn't look like she could be over the age of sixty with short blonde hair and a sleek floor length red dress and matching jacket.

Her mom smiles and immediately her eyes lock onto mine. "So, you're him." Uh oh. "You know, since my husband hired you—twice now—I haven't ever met you face to face, and now here you are, with Scarlett."

I can't tell if this is going to be a good conversation, but I stand anyway and hold out my hand. "Nice to meet you…"

"Karen." She smiles. "You can call me Karen or Kitty for short."

Do not laugh, do not laugh.

"Moooommmmm." Scarlett draws her name out. "No more Kitty, because you know what ends up happening. Dad cracks an inappropriate joke, and everything goes to hell."

"True." She sips her glass of champagne. "I'm genuinely curious, Killian. How long have you guys been dating behind her father's and my back? Since the failed wedding, or is this more recent?"

I'm going to kill Scarlett. "It's newer. I had to get my head together, but it doesn't mean it's not real or deep."

She raises a shaky hand to her face. "Donald, Donald get over here!"

Scarlett's dad rushes over in his black suit and presses a kiss to her cheek. "You look beautiful."

"Thanks, Dad."

"It's real!" Karen giggles. "Just look at the way he looks at her, and oh, my, I knew it. I knew Addison was being a little twat."

Scarlett chokes on her next sip of wine, and I have a sudden urge to pull Karen into my arms and give her a hug.

"Sweetheart!" Donald exclaims through clenched teeth. "Remember, we're on our best behavior for our youngest daughter's wedding."

Karen rolls her eyes. "Doesn't make it any less true. I blame you. You spoiled her all through high school." She waves him off, looking slightly tipsy. "But now that Addison wants to surprise them and make up for it, I don't see why we can't just do it!"

Scarlett leans in and whispers in my ear, "What are we doing?"

"It was Addison's idea." Karen grins. "After all, she ruined the first wedding and now look at her, I think deep down—"

"So very deep." Her dad chimes in.

He gets elbowed again.

Karen rolls her eyes. "Deep down she feels bad and embarrassed it happened that way, I mean, who wouldn't?"

Addison. Addison wouldn't. And I barely know her.

"Anyway, what better way to make up for a failed wedding than throw an impromptu one for you two? I mean, it won't be legal since we don't have the license, but since Adrian's here we thought we could have a small family ceremony, you can say your vows and stay an extra day if your busy rockstar schedule allows it." Her mom is literally beaming, and I'm ready to have a panic attack because I know Addison is doing it on purpose so if I say no, Scarlett loses face, and if I say yes my agent's going to murder me because, you know, Addison would post it everywhere along with whoever else she's going to gossip to around the wedding.

My phone burns in my pocket.

"Um…" It's all I have before Addison grabs a microphone and stares directly at me like she knows and is seconds away from exposing both of us.

I do something any desperate person would do in front of parents.

I pull them both in for a hug and say yes.

I don't even wait for Scarlett to say anything.

"But we need to keep it private. I can't let the press find out, you understand, plus we would never want to take away from Addison's very special day." I lie through my teeth.

"Good for you." Karen taps me lightly on the cheek and leans in. "Your eyes are so green."

Donald reaches for her. "Okay, now that *that's* been settled, we'll go back to our table. Hydrate honey, you need to hydrate."

They walk off.

Scarlett stares me down, a look of total shock on her face. "Are you insane?"

"We're already knee deep. Plus, it's not going to be legal, we don't have to write our names down, we can play it off as a publicity stunt, if need be, but I can also, I think get any guest that stays for the family wedding to sign something legally binding by Dustin, I haven't had a chance to really digest what needs to happen, but she can't win. I refuse it."

Scarlett's eyes light up. "You're so freaking hot for saying that."

I immediately reach for her, ready to kiss her, when Adrian steps between us. "Oh sorry, were you about to fornicate in front of God and everyone?" He takes the free seat and sets his two plates down. Dustin follows.

I reach for Scarlett again, only to have Dustin cockblock me this time. She takes her original seat. I mouth, "Later."

Her cheeks burn bright pink.

God, I could lick right there. How did we go from fighting to this in such a short time? It's just attraction.

And… pity?

No, not pity.

"Damn…" Dustin shakes his head and takes another huge bite while Addison drones on and on in the microphone.

"…Our love wasn't perfect from the start. It was messy, but it was everything and I'm so thankful to be welcomed into this family." She coughs into the microphone and clears her throat. "Anyway, thank you to my gorgeous fiancé for the wedding of my dreams."

Two of his groomsmen are loudly clanging their glasses next to them. They start to kiss, her cheeks are flushed. Huh, maybe she's drunk?

"Seriously, though. What kind of sauce is in this pasta?" A waitress stops by and grabs his empty plate.

"Oh, so glad you like it!" She beams. "It's a new summer favorite."

"I'd marry it," Adrian announces. "I would marry it so hard, to hell with my vows!"

Scarlett reaches for a bite off his plate and covers her mouth with her hand. "That tastes kind of like… seafood."

"Good palette." The waitress winks. "The chef believes adding a bit of shrimp to the sauce gives it a great flavor with the Sauvignon Blanc. Enjoy!"

"No!" Scarlett and I shout once she walks away.

Dustin's fork clatters onto his plate. "You guys scared the shit out of me! I almost wasted pasta!"

"Is this what an orgasm used to feel like?" Adrian examines the pasta and pops another bite in his mouth. "What?"

Scarlett and I can only watch in horror as Addison takes another drink of water, coughs, then reaches for another bite of pasta.

Scarlett starts chugging her wine, finishes it, then sets it down. "Do we go? Do we stay?"

"Do we take out our phones?" I ask. "I got punched earlier, so I'm gonna need to be told how to handle this situation."

"Huh?" Adrian and Dustin both look up.

Dustin finishes his plate. "What situation? The greatness that is this food?"

"Exactly, you guys are being weird."

"Shrimp," Scarlett and I say in unison.

"Adrian! Addison's allergic to shrimp.

Adrian burst out laughing, then coughs into his napkin. "Sorry, that was very satanic of me, but how allergic are we talking? Like we'll need to call the paramedics or she'll just look like she swallowed a balloon and might need a Benadryl."

"Rash. Red face, sadness." Scarlett gulps. "She's going to swell up and develop a rash the day before she gets married." She gasps. "Oh, shit it's starting, look at her cheeks."

"But death is out of the question?" I ask.

Scarlett's eyes widen even further. "Oh, God."

"What's starting? When's it end? I don't like surprises!" Dustin looks around the room. "I'm so confused, and I was so happy with the shrimp."

Adrian makes a cross in front of his chest. "I quite honestly don't know how to feel about this moment. I agree, we need to know if we should say something."

"Bro, do you not see how much pasta was piled up on her plate when we went to the buffet? She was eating while walking."

A sneeze follows. Addison starts coughing again and turns to one of her bridesmaids and motions for more water.

Scarlett winces. "Maybe nobody will notice?"

"Yeah, nobody's going to notice how her cheeks are suddenly puffing up to the size of Flounder. You know she's going to find a way to blame you, right? Even though none of this is your fault and not attempted murder."

Dustin nods. "Should I get the papers?"

I glare. "Stop with the papers. We don't need her to sign a paper saying I'm not an accomplice in her murder, besides we'll just blame you or the priest. You guys were the ones hovering over there and interrupting what I'm sure would have been a heavy amount of groping and kissing over here."

"So heavy," Scarlett agrees. "Okay, I'm going to fall down on my own sword and just go let her know. Pray for me."

Adrian doesn't respond, Dustin's staring on with horror. "I'm gonna go with you."

"You don't have to."

"Yeah, I think I do. I can block any kicks or hits, wouldn't be the first time a woman slapped me."

Adrian snorts. "Wow. so shocking considering your hedonistic lifestyle."

I flip him off and grab Scarlett's arm. Together, we slowly make our way to the main table. The only person paying attention to Addison's horror is the maid of honor, Barb something, who I briefly met while searching for Gertrude. She came on to me like a snack and had such a scary look in her eyes that I sidestepped her and said I had to pee.

"Honey," Barb whispers under her breath. "Do you remember eating anything with shrimp or pine nuts in it?"

"No." Addison's lips look like a botched filler job gone wrong. Her eyes are watering like crazy. "I just ate the pasta! Oh God, what am I going to do?"

"Don't panic, stop panicking. It's fine, we'll get you some allergy medicine. Maybe there's a doctor here—Oh wait! The other groomsman!"

"The one who does coke?"

I cough into my hand. "Um, maybe we can be of service. You see, my assistant asked what was in the pasta, and we just found out there are remnants of shellfish scattered around it."

Addison jumps to her feet. "THEWES NO WAY! I CHECKED THE MENWU!"

I keep my laugh in; it's one of the hardest things I've ever done. "Well, maybe they're wrong, but the evidence is…" I hold out my hand. "Definitely jarring, to say the least."

"It's fine!" Scarlett jumps in. "We'll just find you some Benadryl and ice packs. You'll be totally fine!"

"UW!" Addison jabs a finger in Scarlett's direction. "UW PWOISIONT ME!"

"Yeah, not going great," I whisper under my breath. "Should we go for plan B?"

"I didn't poison you! I've been with this guy the entire time!"

"UW BOTH DID!"

"But can you poison *poison*?" I say so only Scarlett can hear me.

"AGHHHH!" Addison screams and stomps her foot.

"Yeah, definitely plan B." I grab Scarlett's hand and flip her around. "Run!"

We move quickly through the crowds. Addison's still screaming and now throwing what sounds like silverware, and I do what smart men do.

I grab Dustin and yell. "Cover us!"

"Again?" he grumbles. "And if she hits me?"

"Give her a form!" I yell and then me and Scarlett are out, running through the hall and toward our suite.

She's stumbling next to me.

And I may or may not be laughing.

When we finally get back to the suite, I close the doors, lock them, and turn around, only to see Scarlett already taking off her dress.

"Wh-what are you doing?" I'm panting. I'm not sure if it's from the run or if it's because I see bra.

Her dress falls to a pool at her feet, she steps out of it in her red heels and walks toward me.

Mouth dry, I grab her and press a rough kiss to her mouth. "Why am I getting rewarded?"

"Easy." She shrugs a pale shoulder. "You stood by my side."

# TWENTY

## Scarlett

I made the choice the minute he offered to go with me to my evil sister, because what sort of hero actually goes to the villain and says, yeah, I'll play even though I know we're all probably going to die a fiery death; hey, at least we're together.

That's what having him by my side feels like, and I'd forgotten what it was like to have someone you're attracted to, romantically interested in, and sometimes loathe, just ride or die no matter how many times you've argued over the last hour, no matter how many mishaps.

His simple answer was yes.

There was really no explanation.

There was no arguing in the one moment I needed someone to just hold my hand, even though the situation was semi-comical.

Killian's green eyes are wide while he watches me walk

toward him, his full gorgeous lips part, his hands at fists at his sides, fingers moving back and forth between tense and relaxed like he isn't sure if he is allowed to touch when all I want him to do is touch, tug, jerk, slam my body into the nearest wall and lift me up against it.

Romance novels go one of two ways: you have this emotional moment where the people tear up and cry over the sex, or you have the moment where you just get taken. I'm okay with both, or a combo of both, but right now, what I really want is to be lost in him and do something for me.

Maybe that's what empowerment is all about, wanting—no, needing—to take the consequences and make the most of the small moments you're given.

Killian's breathing heavy, his eyes don't take in my body like I thought they would, they're fully trained on mine, half-lidded, his caramel hair is messy from his run.

"Why am I getting rewarded?" he finally asks.

"Easy." I shrug, because it really is such an easy answer. "You stood by my side."

In one stride, he has my elbow in a death grip, his hands are warm, and huge against my arm. He uses his other hand to grip my ass and lift me against him. We're finally alone.

His lips are hot and tender at the same time. Maybe he wants to savor the moment as much as I do. He pulls away lightly, brushing kisses down my jaw and my neck, small nibbles here, bigger bites as with one hand he slowly tugs my bra down, then flicks it completely off.

"Wasting no time?" I ask.

"I've wasted a fucking year," he growls. His answer has me nearly melting on the spot, and I'm already halfway there with the way he holds me. I think back to all our arguments, the sexual tension, being abandoned by him or feeling abandoned when I was in school, only to feel abandoned again on my wedding night, but I shove it all away.

Everyone has their reasons.

The CIA believes that everyone has three lives, I saw a TikTok on it once. The first is the public life you want people to perceive. The next is the private life you tell nobody about, and finally your secret life, with the deepest, darkest parts of your soul you wish to God is never exposed.

I know his public life—I've seen parts of his private life—but he's never shown me his secrets.

I say this as I kiss him harder, as I hold my own secrets and dreams too close, too afraid to share them with anyone for fear of being left. Because if someone claims they'll stay by your side and you show them the good, the bad and ugly, what happens when the ugly is too much to handle? And what happens when you feel that space next to you in bed?

And it's empty, with all your secrets gone and exposed, with that person, forever. You never get them back and you lose that part of your life forever to that person who stole what was so hard to give.

Killian's forehead touches mine roughly before he carries me into the primary bedroom, kicking the door closed behind him with a bang. I'm trying to pull his T-shirt from his head, and finally get it off onto the floor. My hands reach for the button of his dark jeans, but I can't get them off unless he drops me.

He slowly lowers me to the bed; he doesn't toss me, he doesn't cover my body with his and punish me with kisses.

"Is this my reward?" I smile as he slowly pulls down his jeans. Of course rockstar who wears leather pants is completely commando. My eyes widen. I suck in a sharp breath. "Should you be carrying weapons?"

He leans down and presses a kiss to each breast. "I dunno, should you?" He smirks and flicks a nipple. "You know you should get these pierced."

"Why?" I ask, slightly insulted.

"So I can watch"—he grins—"the pain, and then give them all the pleasure they deserve over and over again."

"Sadist?" I inquire.

He kisses my nose. "Only the good kind."

"Didn't know we had those."

His body is heavy, covering mine. "I volunteered as tribute."

His arms brace either side of my body, his biceps swirling with tattoos that hold lyrics, pictures of skulls, one of his album covers with a red umbrella, a dragon, he doesn't discriminate, but I think my favorite one is the one on his chest that says smoke and mirrors.

I trace it with my fingertip. "What's this mean?"

He sighs and kisses me again, not answering me, not allowing me to get a word in edgewise as his tongue slides into my mouth again and again, his hands move to my hips, tugging my thong completely down and dropping them onto the floor. His green eyes blaze as he pulls back and flicks my heels with a finger. "I think I want you to keep these on, I wanna feel the sharp pain of them biting into my skin, with your legs wrapped around me so tight I have bruises."

My lips part at the same time he grabs my ass and tugs me down the bed. He's rock-hard and hot against my stomach. I arch with every kiss up my calve, to my ticklish knees and spread thighs. His hands tug me open.

It's been so long, I whimper before his mouth even descends; his tongue is first followed by his fingers.

Rob seldom did this, and if he did, it was so quick it was like he wanted a high five for giving it the good ol' college try.

"Knew you would taste good everywhere." Killian grunts against me. "It's embarrassing how much I want you."

"It's equally embarrassing"—I pant—"how much I need you."

He continues touching me, teasing me, and pants. "Condom?"

"I trust you."

He stills, his fingers completely stop moving. "Don't."

"Because I didn't sign a paper?" I tease, a bit nervous now.

His green eyes darken as he lightly taps my ass with his right hand. "Don't bring Dustin and his documents into our bed."

Our bed.

Our bed.

I like the sound of it.

"Nightstand," I finally blurt out, embarrassed that I even have them, but I was told manifestation was key when it came to all good things, by a priest friend of mine that I will definitely offer wine and a holiday ham to later.

Killian's golden hair falls over his eyes as his lean body slants across mine, he reaches into the nightstand, grabs one, tears it off with his teeth and slides it on. "Normally I'd apologize for not letting you finish with my mouth first." His grin is wicked. "But I kind of want my dick to be the only thing that has you screaming. He has jealousy issues."

"With just me?"

"Like you have to ask." He kisses me again. I can feel the large tip of him right at my center, teasing me, back and forth, back and forth, like a slow song I never want to end.

"Sing for me." I'd whispered.

But he saved me instead.

He slowly, achingly thrusts in, and my body welcomes him like it's been wanting to since our first kiss in my house, since the first night it started, the first night it ended.

His mouth finds mine while his hands grip my hips and pull me hard against him, slow fluid strokes of his tongue and of his cock are in fluid sync. "I thought rockstars would be more aggressive."

"Did you now?" he whispers against my mouth.

I kick my heels around him and pull him in tight. "Did I say I was disappointed?"

His wince brings more joy than pain as he deepens his thrusts. "Been wanting these legs around me for too many months, dreamt about them at least a dozen times in the last day."

"Even in the shower?" I whimper when he stops.

His eyes narrow. "You saw?"

I bite down on my lower lip. "I watched."

"Fuck me." He pulls out of me and, without asking, flips me onto my stomach. "Grip the headboard."

I grip the black wood while my shoes flip off my feet. He rests his chin on my shoulder and pulls my hair back from my skin. "Did you like it?"

When he enters me again, it's aggressive and punishing.

I moan and grip the wood until my knuckles turn white, his hands find my breasts, squeezing them to the near point of pain. "Answer?"

"Yes," I grunt out. "Yes."

"Me too." He bites down on my shoulder hard enough for me to scream and shoves his palm down the front of my stomach, down between my legs. "Now I get to feel you and watch."

"Yes," I say it again because I can't think of actual words as his rhythm picks up, his body's slamming against me, his palm is rubbing against me and everything feels too good, like a rising crescendo you know will have to end but you'll beg for a repeat.

I lean over, my hair falls across my face and I don't scream, not when I feel my body releasing, not when I feel him tensing behind me, not when I'm staring at the wood headboard and hoping we didn't do permanent damage yet hoping we did.

I stay like that, panting, for I don't know how long he doesn't pull out of me. Instead, his hands move to mine and slowly pry them from the headboard. Still inside me, he falls back against the bed, taking me with him and draws me to his side.

"Let me be here, for just one minute," he rasps.

I want to say stay forever.

Instead, I nod and cuddle back into him.

I sigh and start playing with his hands. He's wearing a few random rings on his right hand, and one on his left where a wedding band would be.

"Not a wedding ring. I could feel you tensing," he whispers into my hair. "It's more or less a reminder."

"Of?" I ask.

"What happens when you give your heart away."

"What's that?"

"Abandonment. Consequences. Betrayal."

"You don't believe in marriage or love?" My heart is breaking for him. I mean, even in my situation, I would try again. I know I would. I want to. Even if I am half broken.

It's his turn to tense. "You know what it's like to have your deepest darkest secret, hold it close, and know there's shame in it, and you tell someone about it and see their eyes flicker with warning and not understanding but almost horror that you never shared in the first place, when the only reason you didn't share was because you were scared?"

Tears well in my eyes. "Actually, yeah, I do, but I don't regret telling my truth even if it was too ugly for them to accept, too heavy for them to carry."

"Hmm, maybe I need to hire you to write me some sad songs."

I elbow him in the abs. "I would be excellent."

He chuckles. "Something tells me you're naturally good at everything, even poisoning people without actually being near food."

"Very funny."

We're in a comfortable silence. He pulls away from me and disposes of the condom, but I don't move until he flips me toward him and starts tracing the side of my hip with his fingertips. "All Smoke, All Mirrors," he says softly, still tracing but not making eye contact. "It means it's all fake, the public persona on stage, it's all to entertain, and to remind me that when the lights go down, and when everyone leaves—because eventually they do, life is lonely, they only want the rockstar, and I don't want to lose myself to stage Killian Stone."

Tears fill my eyes. "Something tells me that's the least of your worries, especially with all your success."

"Ah, stalk me, do you?"

"Yes, I have a shrine built in front of Chuck Norris's tank at home, he too likes to worship. Sometimes I even light a candle, buy the last Rolling Stone, and cut out tiny little pictures. I like to call it my vision board. I asked Adrian to put holy water on it, but he refused."

"Absolute killjoy."

"You're telling me." I laugh. "Hey, thanks for sharing all that."

He wraps his arms around me and kisses me again. I never want him to let go, but people like him are butterflies—they belong in the world to create tiny little flaps of their wings and tiny little moments for people to enjoy forever.

Cutting his wings seems wrong when he could fly so high.

"You're not ordinary," I finally say when we pull apart. "You also drive me crazy. But I like it."

"You're no sunshine either some days."

"Sorry for yelling at you."

"Sorry for yelling back."

I wince. "I might yell more in the next day or so, just a good warning."

"I'll probably secretly like it." He laughs.

My stomach growls instantly.

"Someone hungry?"

"I could use some cheese." I wrinkle my nose. "I was going to have some of the glorious Dateline pasta, but had sex instead."

He grips his chest. "My heart bleeds."

"It was very rough, I don't know how I made it through getting pounded into a headboard like that and having the best orgasm of my life, remind me later to give you a high five or at least a solid pat on the ass."

"I vote pat on the ass."

I laugh again. God, he's so easy, like so easy to be with. I knew that the first day I met him. I know it even more now.

I'll be fine though.

It's always fine.

I have no choice.

He'll go to LA, I'll go back to Seattle, and everything will be… sadly normal. I'll talk about great sex and think only of him, and he'll sing about it and do it for the world.

Yeah, sounds fair.

"Stay here." He kisses me on the forehead and disappears for around five minutes. When he returns, he's holding an open bottle of wine and a board full of cheese, crackers, and fruits. "Gift from your dad. It seemed only fair to celebrate sleeping with his daughter and accepting that gift and giving him a cheers."

"My dad stays out of our room the way Dustin does."

He bursts out laughing, sets everything on the nightstand, then grabs his T-shirt off the floor and slips it over my head, careful to make sure my hair doesn't get tangled, then pulls it out, smoothing it over my back. The shirt's long enough that I really don't need underwear, but he grabs mine anyway and jerks his head toward me.

I stand.

He slowly crouches in front of me, holding them open, and I step into them. When he pulls them all the way up my body, I'm on fire again.

He bites out a curse. "We should eat before I eat again."

"Huh?"

"Now my mouth's jealous." He winks and pulls on his jeans, which barely fit around his dick. "First, we eat."

# TWENTY-ONE

*Killian*

The number of times I curse post sex in my head is alarming. I want to keep her. I'm selfish like that. I told her as much as I felt I could, but even then, I want to open up more, which just reminds me what happened last time I did and the consequences it took on my heart and my band at the time.

I pop a piece of cheese in my mouth, then take a swig of the red wine I found in the kitchen and hand it to Scarlett.

She's gorgeous in my shirt. Damn it, I want to rip it from her. She tilts her head back and takes a swig, then hands it back. "So classy."

"It was this or wake up the guys and try searching for glasses. I was too afraid to go too close to the other guest bedroom."

She laughs and then shushes herself. "Sorry, they're probably completely spent after the day we had."

"You think we should have tucked them in? Told them a nice, non-scary story, mainly for Adrian."

She nods.

"He will dream of Gertrude often."

"I call that a nightmare."

"Bet he's spooning Dustin while Dustin stresses out over forms and tries to deflect calls from my agent."

Her face falls. "Is everything really okay?"

"Yeah." I lie. I hate lying, especially to her. "It's just… her trying to do her job well and reminding me to stay far, far away from scandal."

Scarlett hangs her head. "I may as well have that printed on my face at this point."

I reach for her face and hold it with one hand. "Where? I don't see it. Should I search for it?" I start kissing her mouth again. She tastes like wine, I could drink it from her mouth. She kisses me back and then her eyes move behind me toward the door and widen.

"What? What?"

"Do. Not. Move." She slowly lifts the wine and sets it on the table, but when she picks up the cheese, something must scare her, because she's jumping on top of the bed and reaching for the headboard, trying to climb her way up.

I follow suit. "What the hell is wrong?"

"M-mouse!" She points. "There's a mouse!"

Sure enough, by the door staring at us, and most likely from one of the vineyards outside, is a small field mouse looking innocent as hell, but I know facts because of stupid Dustin.

So I whisper, "They eat their young."

She hits me on the chest. "Why would you choose this time to tell me that?"

"They have supersonic hearing and can fit through a hole the size of a pencil."

I get hit again. "Why do you know this?"

"Because! Dustin!" I yell. "He knows every useless fact and now I wish for once in my life he would have told me if they run at you or if they run away from you!"

"Shoo!" she yells. "Shoo!"

I roll my eyes. "Do you really think he understands English?"

"YES!" She's starting to get hysterical, more than any adult I've seen in the presence of a small rodent.

I turn to her and ask slowly, "Why are you so scared of mice?"

She fidgets a bit with my shirt and mumbles her answer against my shoulder.

She's adorable. I cup my ear. "What was that?"

"I was scared of Gus Gus! Okay?"

I'm so confused. I mean, does she mean...? "The cartoon?"

"It was his laugh, okay?"

I try, I really do, but I start howling with laughter. "This is so sad! It's a fairy tale!"

"So is Hansel and Gretel, and a witch nearly eats them, luring them with candy."

"Uh duh, the moral of the story is don't get into a van when someone offers you candy, it's not free, candy is never free. Just like muscles, gotta work for them."

"AHHH!" She jumps into my arms. "IT MOVED!"

Suddenly Dustin runs into the room in nothing but boxers with The Office printed on them and Adrian follows with black, tight briefs. One has a mop, the other a broom.

Ah, full Cinderella circle.

"What!" Dustin yells. "What is it?"

"Mouse!" Scarlett yells.

"Damn it, she's terrified of Gus Gus!" Adrian yells.

"So your answer was to clean him?" she yells back.

"NOT NOW." He's clearly angry. "I'm thinking, and you know I had a mouse as a pet that died when I was very young! I have trouble killing God's creatures."

"Um…" Dustin looks around. "Where did God's small creature disappear to?"

That's strange, it had just been right by their feet; maybe they scared it away with all the yelling and cleaning. Adrian does a small turn, and so does Dustin, before facing us again.

The mouse is literally so small it's on the front of his boxers and he can't even tell that tiny creature is officially the O in The Office. On. His. Boxers.

I'll never watch that show the same again. Dustin ruins everything. He really does.

Scarlett's eyes go wide, but she doesn't scare Dustin by pointing. Adrian follows her line of vision, holding his mop out like a sword. "Dustin, I need you to be very still."

"Huh? What? Why?" His hands are up like he's getting arrested.

"Shh, shh, shh." Adrian moves the mop up and down like he's getting ready to golf a ball because, well, technically… two of them if he misses. "I'm just gonna scare it."

"You're scaring ME!" Dustin squeals as he looks between us. "Why is everyone staring at my dick? Guys, I like The Office, sue me. It's my only solace after working in one for so long and wanting to bang my head between the doors. I shouldn't have to look forward to donut day. That's just sad."

"Shhhhhhh, it's gonna be okay," Adrian says in a calming tone, ah the priest has arrived. "I'm just going to scare him from the front of your pants. He'll shimmy down your leg and then we can safely escort him outside. Killian, carefully go to the sliding glass door and open it, try to maneuver it outside."

I get off the bed and open the door wide.

"Now Dustin, walk without fear toward that door."

Dustin starts walking, but the mouse starts to move a bit. At this rate, Dustin will really only have one golf ball. He's one bite away from the ER; I think the closest hospital is at least twenty miles away, too.

"Never mind, bad idea." Adrian shakes his head. "I'm sorry, man, I'm gonna have to hit it at a particular angle to get it to go toward the door, okay?"

Dustin glares at Adrian. "No, not okay. Never okay. I want children someday."

"One." Adrian ignores him and swings. "Two." He nods in finality. "Three."

The mop goes flying toward Dustin's junk, then magically the little parts of it pull the mouse toward me like little tentacles, it does a small turn and with Adrian's majesty he shoves it out the door.

I close it fast and lean against it, wincing. "Man down."

Dustin's holding his balls with his hand. "How does a mop hurt?"

I frown. "Hey, let me see that."

Adrian tosses it. "Why?"

I catch it and check it out. "Oh, I need a good mop, solid brand this one. I'll take a screenshot later."

"Does anybody care about my balls?" Dustin rolls onto his side.

"It was soft, you're fine, get up, have some cheese." I roll my eyes. "I'll get you some ice, though, for your trouble. Hey, good thing it was attracted to your balls, you helped trap it!"

"Yes." Dustin waves from the floor. "Let's celebrate my ability to trap mice in my pants."

Scarlett starts laughing behind her hand, then stops when Dustin glares. "I'll just... um, go grab you something."

"For the love of God, put on pants!" Adrian yells. "Besides, do you realize how thin these walls are?"

"It's the cement." Dustin heaves from the floor like he's seconds away from puking and attracting the mouse again. "It makes all the tragic sounds echo."

"Tragic?" I ask.

"Lots of moaning." Adrian shoots me a glare. "And we know you weren't in here watching Batman."

"That would be the weirdest bedroom game ver." I think about it a minute. "Or maybe the best?" Because Cosplay?

"Whatever." Adrian points his finger at me. "Us. We're talking later."

I feel like I'm getting ready to get sent to detention, or maybe just hell.

Scarlett makes her way back into the room. "Here's some ice, Dustin—"

Adrian grabs her by the arm.

"Okay, I guess I'll be right back."

Dustin sits up, ice on his shorts. "I just have one question."

"No, Dustin, she didn't sign the form."

"I was going to ask if you had any wine left over."

"Oh." I quickly grab it for him and hand it over. He stares at me from his angle on the floor. "What?"

"Don't get her pregnant, all right?"

I laugh, but inside I'm dying. Inside, my heart squeezes a little and whispers bitterly, *don't worry.*

I can't.

Because I'm sterile.

# TWENTY-TWO

*Scarlett*

Adrian takes a deep breath and sits outside on one of the cushy green chairs arranged around the fire pit. He turns the flame on and rubs his hands over it after throwing on a white t-shirt and staring into the fire. Why do I feel like he's about to preach to me right now?

Maybe I'm just being paranoid, but I know all his faces. This one is a mixture of concerned and pensive and something else I haven't seen in a long time.

Is he… jealous?

"Adrian?" I scoot my chair over. "Thinking about jumping into the fire or performing an exorcism? I didn't bring any holy water, but I can watch."

He hangs his head in his hands and groans, then turns to me, his hands still bracing his head, the firelight glowing across his masculine yet pretty features. His jaw is so precise it's almost unreal. "Why him?"

I jerk back. "Why him what?"

"Why that guy?" He points behind him. "I really want to know. Because he's going to leave you, he's not going to stay, and you're going to be heartbroken again, and then where does that leave me? At your house making sure you eat, making sure you go to work. You were heartbroken last time, and you never even told me why.

I look down at my hands. Why are they shaking? "Adrian, I'd just threw my entire life away, found out my entire life was shifting, including my relationship with my sister, my parents, and when I asked for a lifeline, he gave me one, and I think when you're so desperate and someone sees it in your eyes like he's experienced it before over and over again, something in your soul just clicks, something in both of us just clicked. He turned a horrible situation into something that had me laughing by the end of the night, before crying after he kissed me and left. It didn't help that I, um, got sent something in the mail soon after saying I'd be sued if I ever disclosed any information about our hours together."

Adrian leans back in the chair. "You know he probably didn't send that, don't you?"

I sigh. "Yeah, I know that now. Clearly, Dustin's the form guy."

We both share a smile.

"But still." I shrug and cross my arms, then shiver a bit.

Adrian gets up and grabs one of the red plaid blankets from the area by the outdoor couch and brings it over, wrapping it around my shoulders. "Better?"

I nod. "Mm. Yeah."

"But still?" His jaw flexes like he's bracing himself.

"He never came back," I admit. "And it stung because I

was so lost in that moment, I thought he'd at least text or say something, ask if I was okay, something. And then he became even more famous, and I chalked it up to a coincidence, or maybe serendipity, that he was there and I was there, but now..." I look over my shoulder. "You should know, we used to know each other briefly when we were kids. I didn't figure it out because he'd changed his name. He has a stage name, and I only knew him nine months before he left for the UK after his parents' divorce. He promised to message me, and email and he never did, and I lost his information in a freak washing machine accident. I just assumed he'd connect with me, but he left me. Then he left me a second time, but I still have feelings for him, and even if that means I have tonight, tomorrow. Why can't I have that?"

"Third time isn't always a charm, Scar."

I softly punch his shoulder. "Aren't priests supposed to be optimistic?"

He looks away from me, his cheeks going red. "Yeah, we're supposed to be a lot of things, apparently." He licks his lips. "You never asked, you know, why I became a priest."

I tilt my head. "I guess it just never came up. After we rekindled our friendship, you were already a priest, and I was already broken."

"You were never broken, just a bit damaged, like a bird who—"

"Loses its wings?"

"Hell, no." He laughs. "I'm not that cheesy. I was going to say like a sad little baby bird that gets kicked out of the nest and is forced to fly, but goes splat over and over again."

"Encouraging. I can see why your congregation loves you."

He lets out a belly laugh. "Oh yeah, it's definitely because they don't like my good looks. Riveted, they're riveted."

"The deep voice helps." I put my hand on his forearm; he reaches over and covers it with his. It's warm, comforting.

His eyes flicker down to my mouth.

I don't know what's happening, but the firelight under the moon makes it feel dangerous. I start to slide my hand away, but he grips it firm. "We broke up, because I was an idiot, and when I finally got up enough courage to reach out a few months later, you were already dating someone else, and then in a whirlwind of announcements, you were engaged."

"I was heartbroken," I say simply. "And then some rich good-looking guy came along and treated me like glass, which I recently discovered is the worst possible thing ever and people like that should be kicked in the balls."

"Repeatedly," he agrees.

"And it felt like a fairy tale, and I was just getting over the darkness. I felt fulfilled and happy, and I wasn't scared anymore or sad. He treated my family amazingly, and I fell hard and fast. I imagine this is how it feels to be conned? Anyway, he helped me get over you in the way I needed."

"Wow." Adrian drops my hand and looks away, then stands and starts pacing. "Are you telling me had I been a few weeks earlier? A month? That we'd be together right now?"

I frown. "Adrian, that's not how the universe works."

He kicks the chair next to him and tears at his hair. "Fuck!"

I jump a foot. He has his hands on his hips now and he's looking away from me like he can't bear to look at me.

"Adrian?"

He turns abruptly. "You always told me to follow my heart, and I was so fucking heartbroken that I followed my stupidass sister to her church, and I finally felt good about something about a purpose. I went into seminary that next week after graduation."

My stomach drops. "Are you saying you became a priest…" I can't say it, I can't breathe the words out loud.

"Ironic." He stares up at the sky again. "Wow."

"You're angry."

"Of course I'm angry, Scarlett!"

"Please don't yell," I whisper.

"Sorry." He squeezes his eyes shut. "Sorry, I'm not angry at you. I'm angry at myself, and maybe at the universe and the way it works."

I stand and walk over to him, grabbing his arm. "Hey, this is how things were supposed to work out, right?"

He stares back down at me… I always forget how tall he is, how muscular. He swallows and shakes his head, and his eyes are lost before they fall to my mouth again.

No. No. I will not lose my best friend.

I slowly back away, but he jerks me against him, chest heaving.

"You made vows," I whisper. "And I'm with someone else."

"Vows can be broken, and not for long."

I jerk away. "That's cruel. That's not you speaking."

"It is." He jerks up his chin. "It really is."

"You're talking out of anger and reacting. The past is in the past. Don't, please don't do something that will make me lose you again."

He grabs my hand and slowly tugs me forward again. "Would it be so bad to love me?"

I smile. "I already do, just not the way you want me to, and not the way you love your job. Even you can't deny that. You'd resent me. Eventually, you'd leave too. I can't handle you leaving." I start to cry. "I can't imagine you leaving me again."

"Scar…" Tears fill his eyes. He pulls me against him in a tight hug and starts running a hand down the back of my head, holding it against his chest. "You won't. You won't lose me, I'd cut my own heart out before that."

"Gory."

"You know how I feel about Scream."

I laugh against his chest. "Please don't let this come between us, don't draw lines in the sand, let me live my present and future, the way you should too."

"Wise words." He sighs and draws away from me. "I um, I'm going to go take that walk you talked about." Tears glisten in his eyes, his smile's forced. "I'll be back. Promise I won't get attacked by a cougar, okay?"

"Pftt, you'd kill it."

He's already turned around but calls over his shoulder. "God's creatures."

"It probably ate that mouse!" I yell.

He looks over his shoulder and gives me a sad smile, then grabs a pair of flip-flops from outside, wraps a blanket around his shoulder, and walks.

My legs are shaking by the time he's gone around the corner. I can barely stand. I think I might also throw up.

I love him as a best friend.

We were immature when we were together. But we're the perfect match—as friends now.

Please don't let someone else walk out. Why can't anyone

stay? Why can't someone stay by my side? And why do I get ignored when I beg to stay by theirs?

It's hard to swallow, it hurts to hold in tears right now.

When I'm just about to break, strong arms wrap around me from behind, a chin rests heavily on my head. I know his smell, I know the way his hands feel around my body, the way his body feels inside mine.

"You okay?" he whispers.

I swallow a few times before inhaling his scent and answering. "Maybe. I don't know. How much did you hear?"

He squeezes me tighter, wrapping the blanket around me warmly. "The man literally went outside without pants. If I have to put on pants, he has to put on pants, so I went searching for the ugliest pair I could find in his luggage which weirdly enough I also own the same pair of, and was gonna knock and just drop them, then I heard some things, and then I stayed, I'm sorry. I just… I got jealous and then I stayed longer because I could hear your heart breaking in the wind and I hated it."

"You can't hear hearts break, it's silent, only painful for the ones experiencing it."

"You can hear it when you care for someone, like a twig snapping in the distance, like something final," he whispers. "If you want to be alone, tell me. If you want to watch the stars, tell me. If you want me to hold you, tell me. And if you want me to sing you a song… tell me."

A tear slides down my cheek as I turn in his arms and whisper, "Sing for me."

Why does it feel so final? Like this might be the last time?

He nods slowly and lightly cups my cheeks. "There once was a ship…"

I burst out laughing. I laugh so hard I break apart from him. "You ass! You would start singing Wellerman! You're the worst."

"Hey." He pulls me close against his chest. "In my book, I made you laugh instead of cry, that makes me the best."

My cheeks hurt from smiling. "Think so, huh?"

He leans down and steals one kiss, then two. He tastes like whiskey and all the bad choices I want to make because somehow everything with him has turned to good. He only draws back a bit. "Yeah, I do think so."

"She needs to sign a document!" Dustin yells from the sliding glass door.

I don't even look. "Does he still have ice on his balls?"

Killian nods. "It's hard to watch. He has wet spots now, making them slightly see through."

I make a face. "That would kill any erection."

"His or mine?"

"Ewwwww, everyone's!"

"Ah well, I have the girl I like standing out with me in the moonlight. I'm not sure what could kill that erection."

"Dustin?"

"I've learned to ignore the screaming." His forehead touches mine. "Want to go inside or stay out here?"

I look around, my eyes landing on the couch. "I'd actually like to stay out here."

He starts to pull away, his face falls.

I tug at his hand. "But with you. And a blanket, and wine, and possibly a bit of kissing."

He spins me in a circle. "You know rockstars have zero self-control."

I start laughing. "You are the epitome of control these

days. Why not just take me up against the wall and have your way with me, dirty little rockstar?" I'm just teasing... well, kind of.

But something flashes in his eyes before he picks me up and walks me over to the couch. "Dustin, turn off the lights, look away, nurse your broken dick. I'm about to use mine."

Dustin sighs and lowers the paper. "They're all the same, they think the same, oh I'm the talent, I can do whatever I want, just pay them off, just look the other way, just let me do what I want. Who do you work for?"

Killian frowns and looks behind him. "When have I ever said that to you?"

"Oh, not you, you just get mad about the random dinosaur facts and my inability to stop talking when I'm uncomfortable." He clears his throat.

Killian clears his.

"Have a good night." Dustin abruptly closes the door, the outdoor lights are off, and all we have is the moonlight and the fire.

I know Adrian's off on his walk.

And here I am, in this spot with Killian.

I like him. I really, really like him. He's a man I could love, but I would be too afraid to admit it out loud. That's like jumping into the nearby gorge and hoping not to drown in the Columbia River.

Killian leans down on his elbows and kisses me. He's so easy to fall for; I dig my hands into his thick hair. "I like you."

His smile doesn't leave his face, it just gets bigger. "I like you too."

I lick my lips. "Why did you leave so abruptly? Back then?"

His smile falls immediately. "My parents divorced, and I had to go back to the UK with my dad for some things."

"What things?" I lean up on my elbows. "To help with the divorce?"

He hesitates and then answers. "Yeah, it was hard for him, really hard."

"And you too." I cup his face. "I'm sorry I wasn't there."

"Well, you're here now."

I wrap my arms around his neck, then press my lips to his pulse. His heart is beating so fast I can feel it vibrate through my lips. That makes two of us. "You can kiss me now, Killian."

He pulls the blanket back over us and hovers over me. "I guess the big question is, do I have to stop?"

"If I say never?"

"Then I'll say, give us right now."

My heart shakes a bit at that answer, but I promise it we'll be okay this time, so I nod my head yes as his head descends. A few more days and this amazing man won't belong to me anymore.

No, he'll belong to the world.

To his fans.

And I'll have to move on knowing that I at least had a few moments where someone like him held my hand, made me laugh, cry, and gave me memories I'll never forget.

I won't beg him to stay either.

I won't count the seconds, mash them into minutes, hours, days, then stare at the clock when I know it's time.

Killian ducks his head under the blanket. Before I know it, I'm completely bare to him, he shoves his tongue into me, stars explode in the sky and inside me, he's carrying me until the end, his hands digging into my thighs, the imprint of his rings on my skin, the feel of his hot wet mouth working me the way I've always dreamed of, the pleasure and pain of wanting to jump into the abyss yet wanting to stay in the moment forever.

It feels like the beginning of the end. I move my hips slightly with the rhythm of his tongue and then his fingertips as he dials my body in.

A tear slides down my cheek.

I ignore it.

Tears will do nothing in this situation.

My body explodes with pleasure, then stills when his hands spread me wider until I can't breathe. His hair tickles the sides of my thighs. I try to reach for his head, to pull him up, to feel him everywhere, but he doesn't budge, he latches on.

One hand reaches up to slap a hand over my mouth. I'm confused until his other hand replaces his tongue, and I let out a scream that would have most definitely brought on all the mice and cougars. I bite into his palm, legs shaking, he rewards me by biting and then sucking the inside of one thigh, then the other.

I'm panting when he finally removes his hand from my mouth.

I hate that when he locks eyes with me, he looks devastated.

So I grab his face with both hands and pull him in for a kiss. "Maybe we can both be stars tonight?"

He looks up. "You mean like we can both be rockstars or live under the stars?"

I slowly move him off me and push him against the couch, then crawl onto him.

His eyes are wild, like the wilderness around me.

I tug his jeans down and pull him free.

He curses and squeezes his eyes shut. "No, you don't have to—"

"Have to do what? I was just giving you some air."

He opens one eye, suspicious. "Giving my dick some air, huh? Never heard that one."

"Well now you have." I grip him hard, sending his hips toward me, and then I lower my head while he watches with anticipation, before I duck under the blanket.

He tugs it away. "No. I get to watch you suck me. I get to see your eyes every time I go too deep, every time you choke on me, every time you pleasure me. I own it, because you're mine, don't take it away from me."

I smile with sadness in my soul. "I won't."

He's so huge I have to focus, and he's gripping the blanket like he might die from trying not to finish.

I pull up and stare at him, cupping him. "You can let go, you know."

His nostrils flair. "Easier said than done."

"With me," I say. "You can let go with me."

"And if you leave me?"

"Why would I?"

"Broken people can only be broken so many times, Scar."

I lower my head again and finish him off, sucking down every last part of him, before locking eyes with him. "Maybe if you find matching pieces in someone else—you'll be whole again."

I spend the rest of the night under the stars with Killian holding me, and the universe watching.

And me waiting for a shooting star I can wish on, just so I can stay like this forever.

I don't see one.

Then realize maybe the star I need to wish on is right next to me. So when he's sleeping, I press a hand to his chest where his heart is, and whisper, "Stay."

# TWENTY-THREE

*Killian*

I get ready for the wedding slowly because I know once their wedding ends, our little impromptu fake vow exchange begins, and that seems like the most painful thing that could happen before actually leaving.

I could stay with her for a few days, but she'd want to know more. She'd want to know the reasons I want to run in the other direction, the actual fear I have in my soul. It's why I write music, to get rid of the pain, to push through the chaos of knowing that you might lose and knowing that if you make that bet, your exact future might be that same pain you're trying to escape.

Adrian didn't get back until the morning. He quietly got ready for the wedding, and I quietly put on a nice jacket while Scarlett scrambled around the room in search of her other shoe.

Things definitely escalated last night.

We brought the party from outside to inside, and well, around two a.m., I was like, "I need more."

She pressed her ass against me, and I was gone, so long gone. We had sex two more times before I pretended to go to sleep. At this rate, she'll become an addiction I can't get rid of, something that stains my soul in a way I want to keep blood red.

I look over my shoulder. Scarlett's found the shoe and I see a vision of her constantly looking for things in my house, hell, even throwing that shoe at me. I close my eyes and I envision the best-case scenario.

Survival, meaning staying with her, but I can't give her what she needs, and she doesn't even know it. That I'm half a man, or at least I feel that way, because that's what I was told over and over again before I was left.

*"Killian, you should have told me before I got invested! How could you do this to us? To me? You know that's what I've always wanted! You lied!"*

*Tears fill my eyes. "There are options, we can do so much. I just didn't want to keep it from you." I finger the ring in my pocket for a bit, a gorgeous three karat princess cut diamond I knew she was staring at earlier. "I just wanted to be upfront with you before—"*

*Tears stream down her cheeks. "Before what? You lied again? Before you told me it would be okay after years, hearing over and over again that my dream—" She starts sobbing. "You know how I felt about this, and you still kept it from me this long."*

*The ring drops from my fingers deeper into my pocket, maybe it fell completely through, I don't even know. I just stare at her, hoping she'll realize how much I love her, how much I want to spend my life with her no matter what.*

"No." She lifts her chin. "You lied, and I can't be with a liar, on top of that. It was the one thing, the one thing I spent years talking about, dreaming about, and you still never said anything. You know, I always wondered." She stares down at the ground. "I just thought the odds were in our favor while we dated but, never mind, no, I just—Killian I can't, not right now. I need time."

I stood still.

I watched her give me her back and walk away, and I felt my heart crack in my chest, and the hard part was that it wasn't fast. It didn't drop like I was jumping out of a plane; it was slow, so achingly slow, I would take a step and pain would hit, I would take another, and I would feel a piece shatter against the ground, someone would smile at me, I would smile back, and another piece would crumble because how dare they be happy right now? In my moment of desperation and illusion? I walked up the path; I walked back to a bench, and I sat, and I stared. I knew the ring was still there. I tried texting her; I tried calling.

And the only response I got was, "I can't. I'm sorry. I love you. Goodbye."

After that, my number was blocked.

Just like that, I was blocked. For exposing my truth, I was forgotten. It took months, but eventually I took that same ring and grabbed a hammer. I thought it would satisfy my soul, instead it just made me feel sick. Emotionally, she'd broken me, so physically, I would break what we had.

I didn't feel better.

I felt worse.

Because what we had, I thought at the time, was sacred, precious, once in a lifetime and then in a moment of confessions.

Nothing.

How strong can love possibly be if a few words make someone give you her back? If it takes her from your side in an instant?

I hang my head and watch Scarlett shimmy into her beautiful midnight green gown. It has a plunging neckline, and the back is completely bare. The parts of the skirt dance around her hips and fall to the ground. It's simple, elegant. It matches my eyes.

I get up. "Need me to help zip you?"

She looks over her shoulder, her smile so easy and loving. "Please?"

I can't get the words out, but I want to so desperately. To tell her how I feel, I don't just like her, I wish I did. But something else is there, and I know in the end both of us will get hurt, so I wordlessly walk over to her and touch the zipper at the bottom of her back and zip it up a few inches, then pull her against me. "You're beautiful."

"Says the guy I puked on."

"I'd fucking catch your puke if I had to," I admit honestly. Not the most romantic thing I've ever said, but it doesn't make it any less true.

How did I walk away the first time?

How the hell am I going to do it now?

Scarlett turns and stands up on her tiptoes. "I feel like that's really sweet and gross at the same time. I promise I'll stay away from the whiskey tonight."

I nod. "Just don't stay away from me."

Her eyes search mine as she wraps her arms around my neck. "Killian, where else would I go?"

*Away,* I want to say. Instead, I pull her close and press a kiss to her pink mouth. "Nowhere. You're mine. I decide your future and right now it includes holding my hand in one, a glass of champagne in the other and getting through this wedding, okay?"

She laughs. "Okay, hey don't you need to go rehearse?"

I shrug. "I did a soundcheck when you were sleeping. I'm good, plus, something tells me that the least of our worries is me getting through eight tracks."

She rolls her eyes. "Don't I know it. All right, let's do this."

"Let's." I grip her hand.

Adrian suddenly bursts through the door in none other than a clerical collar. "Holy shit."

I stumble back a step. "Why are you wearing that?"

"Why?" His eyes are wild. "Why? Do you have any idea what happened last night? They can't find the original minister, so here I am! And I bring it everywhere I go, kind of like a bat cape, swear on my life if you make fun of this, I'll murder you and send you to Hell." Bro is aggressive this evening. "And you!" He points at Scarlett. "Why didn't you tell me that the one groomsman, the one with the whiskey, left with some girl and is also missing, so we're short one groomsman."

Scarlett shakes her head. "How do you even know all of this?"

Adrian pauses and looks down at his hands. "I like my morning walks, overheard a few things, then your mom— weirdly strong like Gertrude—pulled me into the field and told me I had one job, perform the wedding, get them married and then she promised wine, so I said yes, pulled out my bat suit…" He glares at me. "…and came back here to report, do you think Dustin would be okay with standing in?"

"Standing?" Dustin yawns and walks in. He's wearing his black shirt and black slacks, but his eyes look swollen, so swollen I can barely see them. "Man, do you guys have bad allergies up here, or is it just me?"

I elbow Scarlett. "You tell him."

She smacks me in the arm. "You tell him."

"I'm a priest, I'll tell him." Adrian grips Dustin's shoulders. "How many fingers am I holding up?" He holds up two.

Dustin shakes him off. "Four. Everyone knows two plus two."

Adrian sighs. "Did you bring your allergy pills?"

"How did you know I have allergies?" He scratches his face vigorously. "Man, it's so dry here."

I wince. "Um, maybe just go take one real quick? Couldn't hurt."

"Probably won't help either," Adrian says under his breath.

Dustin yawns. "I mean, I feel fine. I just need to go do my hair, had the best nap outside, the wind felt amazing."

"Yup. Yup. Yup." Scarlett nods her head. "I'm sure it did."

Dustin smiles, it makes his puffyish face look worse. "I need nature, you know? You know how you just need the outdoors?"

"Every day." Adrian.

"All the time." Scarlett.

"Yup." Me, I got nothing.

Dustin yawns again. "Anyway, I'll just go finish up real quick."

He walks off.

Adrian crosses his arms. "In three, two, one—"

"Holy mother of God!" Dustin shrieks.

I nod. "There it is."

He comes running out of the bathroom and nearly hits the door. "What fresh hell is this? What sort of outdoors am I experiencing? This isn't normal."

No, no it is not.

He pats his face. "I need my pills. I need to find my pills!"

He runs out again.

"So," Scarlett says. "Safe to say, Dustin is most likely out."

They both turn to me.

I glare. "Guys, I'm not going to be a groomsman."

A knock on the door sounds; it's vigorous, angry. I stalk over and jerk it open, only to see Rob on the other side. "Um, hi, look man, I don't normally ask for favors, but, I'm sure you've heard about last night and we need a groomsman and you're probably the only person who can fit into the tux and I um…" He looks down at his shiny black shoes. "Do you think you could possibly just stand in for us? I would really appreciate it and owe you huge."

Like he could afford me.

I look over my shoulder. Scarlett's face is pale. It's like a repeat of her wedding, the chaos, the confusion.

I grab the garment bag from him. "I'll be there in five."

He sighs in relief. "Thank you. Addison's been crying all

morning, with the whole allergic reaction then this. It's been a rough few hours."

"I bet." I want to strangle him. Cheater assface. "I'll show up, but it's only because Scarlett would want that for her sister."

He jerks up, his face sad. "I know. I know she would."

"Don't be an ass," I add. "To Addison, to Scarlett, whatever, just don't be an ass, Rob."

He actually chuckles. "I'm working on it."

"Work harder." I smile. "I'll be there in five."

"We're in the lobby waiting for family pictures."

I hang my head. "Seriously? I have to be in pictures?"

He just shrugs and walks off.

I shut the door and turn.

Dustin, Adrian, and Scarlett are all staring at me in shock. I get ready to say something when Scarlett runs up to me and pulls me in for a hug, the garment bag stands between us. "That was so nice despite the horribleness, thank you."

"Well." I pull back and hold up the bag. "At least we'll be chaos free as long as Adrian doesn't shit his pants at the altar."

Dustin laughs. "Well, he did have the shrimp so…"

"Really? Now?" I roll my eyes. "Let me just change into what will possibly be an entirely too big or small suit and we can all head over."

I manage to fit into the suit in record time and take a look in the mirror. I literally will have to adjust my junk in the blue trousers, but I figure people will be staring at Addison anyway.

I walk out of the bedroom and nearly run into Scarlett. She adjusts the collar of my white shirt and looks down.

Hell, if she does that long enough, I'll have even more inches to adjust.

"I like it." She smiles up at me. "I'll only kiss you once. Promise."

I want to ask her to kiss me more. To stay with me. Instead, I just lean down and kiss her first. "Dibs."

"On my mouth?"

I rub my thumb across her lower lip. "On you."

Her eyes well with tears. "Deal."

This is hard.

This will get harder.

We hold hands and walk with the guys to the main area for the ceremony. Pictures are being held after which means I'll have to stay later, but guests are already arriving at the small venue outdoors. It's beautifully surrounded by vineyards and flowers. Around a hundred and fifty white chairs are placed near more orchids and roses lining the aisle to the different shaped candles in front. Honestly, I'm shocked it's so simple and pretty.

Not at all like Addison.

The minute we make it through the crowd of guests arriving I see Addison—her swelling's gone down, and she's wearing a simple white gown that has white overlay lace all over it with tiny pieces of pink petals stuck into the bottom. It's scrappy and really simple, yet again, not expected. Her hair's hanging over her shoulders and she has a halo like flower thing on her blonde head.

She sees me and beams. "FINALLY!"

Adrian leans in. "Why does that 'finally' make me feel like you're about to lose a testicle?"

I cringe. "Right?"

Dustin holds up a hand.

I slap it away. "No forms needed."

He clears his throat. "It's always good to check."

I roll my eyes and approach Addison. "All right, so where do you need me?"

Her smile is cruel, punishing, she looks between me and Scarlett. "You both look great together, you know that?"

"Thank you?" Scarlett shares a confused look with me.

"But…" Addison grabs my arm. "I had to bring in another bridesmaid too, so I'm gonna just let them get to know each other real quick, so it's not weird."

Scarlett shrugs. "Whatever you want, it's your day."

"Oh, wait!" Addison laughs. "She's right here!" She taps the woman, so that she turns around. She has jet-black hair, crystal blue eyes, and is clearly pregnant. "Thank you so much, Cassidy, for stepping in for me, and thank you for accepting my invitation last week on such short notice."

I have no words.

I have nothing.

I can't imagine the level of conniving it took for this to even happen.

I simply stare at her swelling belly and then look into her eyes.

Cassidy's smile is sad. "Hi, Killian, it's been a while."

Adrian frowns. "You two already met?"

"Oh, yes. Crazy story!" Addison claps her hands together. "They were together for like years. Okay bye, gotta go add more lipstick. If you two could go to the back, the coordinator will tell you when to go down. Thanks again!"

She leaves.

And I'm left with my pregnant ex.

# TWENTY-FOUR

## Scarlett

don't know what to do. I don't know how to respond right now. His ex? And she's pregnant?

Dustin sits down next to me, waiting for the wedding to start. He mumbles under his breath, "I've never seen her form."

I try to get my own breathing under control, but both my rocks are off. One's doing the wedding to my evil sister and the other's talking to his pregnant ex. I have no paper bag and I'm just sitting.

I lock eyes with Adrian; his contain understanding but no anger. The music starts, and he stares at me with intent and mouths. "It's okay."

I shake my head.

He nods his and smiles. "It's okay."

But it's not okay.

The entire wedding procession is a blur to me. I see my

dad give Addison to Rob and I watch in slow motion as they stand the way I stood a year ago.

I need a lifeline.

I need help.

I'm starting to inhale too much air. Killian's up there standing next to the rest of the wedding party looking perfect, and I'm sitting here thinking I might die of a heart attack.

I try to slow my breathing when Dustin reaches his hand across and holds mine. "One, two, three, four, five," he whispers. "Now exhale, one, two, three, four, five." He breathes with me and whispers, "One more time. One, two, three…"

I follow every instruction as Adrian speaks.

Dustin squeezes my hand. "Also, just so you're aware, Killian's not that kind of guy. He would never be with someone then have a one-night stand. He never has. I can't remember the last woman he was with until you."

A tear slides down my cheek. "She's pregnant."

"Right, but that doesn't mean anything."

But it does.

Even if it doesn't.

It's a sad reminder.

Of my past, my future.

Of his.

I sit through the beginning of the ceremony, holding Dustin's hand in a solid grip that will probably cause bruises.

Adrian keeps looking over at me when the vows start.

Addison clears her throat and starts hers. "Rob, I knew you were mine the moment I met you. We were destined to be together. I'll love you forever and never betray you, never leave you, never escape our holy vows. Amen."

Rob smiles. "Addison, you've been the star in my eyes for an eternity, you're glorious in the way you handle life and look at it as a journey you want to spend with not only me but the world. I can't imagine my life without you."

Mikey, one of the groomsmen, laughs under his breath. "Did last night."

Clearly, he's drunk.

My eyes widen. What is happening?

Rob laughs at him. "Ignore him."

"Yeah, okay." Mikey laughs again. "Go ahead, priest."

"Wait." Addison presses Rob's chest with her fingertips. "Don't tell me you actually went along with it!"

Rob sighs. "Can you let it go?"

"NO!"

"It's not like you didn't run off with Mikey the minute I ran off with Barbara. We said this is an open marriage, so leave it!"

My jaw drops.

Addison screeches. "You promised to wait until after the wedding!"

"And that didn't stop you from thrusting your tongue down his throat!" Rob yells.

"I was drunk!" She wails. "And high on Benadryl."

"High enough to do that?" He points at Mikey, good-looking guy, but definitely swaying to the music in his own head.

Addison tosses down her bouquet. "That's it, this wedding is off!"

Holy Wattpad drama!

"Fine, I'll just go find another bridesmaid."

"And I'll find another groomsman!"

"I'll do it better!" Rob yells.

She gasps and slaps him across the face. "What we have is sacred!"

"That's why I love you!" he yells again.

What is seriously happening here?

Dustin just shakes his head. "You see, there's a reason we have a form policy at the agency. Truly, it saves people from getting hit repeatedly, and in Rob's case, from losing his balls altogether."

Addison throws herself at Rob and kisses him. "I just want you!"

"I want you!"

"Um…" Adrian raises his hand. "Then shall I continue, or do we need to go to confession?" He looks so frustrated, I'm afraid he's going to cuss while holding his Bible. His smile is so fake it hurts my face to watch.

Addison fixes her hair, then twists it around her finger. "Sorry, yes, please, we just, um, a rough night with the almost murder, with the mixture of medicine and too much wine. We're ready."

The rest of the wedding goes by fast, thank God, though I see both my parents make a quick escape to the wine table and grab a bottle each once everyone is excused to go to the reception. I don't blame them.

Addison is Rob's issue now.

I stay in my seat even though everyone's allowed to leave, and I watch as they all file out, and then I wait for it.

I wait for the start of the music.

And start it does, followed by Killian's intense voice, singing about going until the end, never leaving someone's side. It's hypnotic.

I sit there through one song, then another.

I remember our laughter. I remember our fights and want to smile even harder. I remember the brief moments in his arms.

And then I remember the darkness when he left last year, how it felt like a torrent of rain, and how I always thought it was because of Rob.

But now I know.

It was because of the star I wished on.

Killian Stone.

I squeeze my eyes shut and feel a hand on my shoulder, and then it reaches for my hand. I look up and it's Adrian.

Then, on the other side, Dustin grabs my other hand. We sit and stare at the emptiness, the place where the bride and groom stood, now bare.

And I remember how it felt to be alone, almost like a bride left at the altar.

Stay by my side. My heart begs.

When my brain knows. Everything has an end.

# TWENTY-FIVE

## Killian

'm not feeling any of the songs, and Cassidy said she wanted to talk after my first and only set, I committed to eight songs total. I'm nearing the eighth and I still don't see Scarlett anywhere.

My heart sinks deeper the more I think about it. She's going to assume the worst and while I want to go strangle the bride, I found out through a brief talk with Cassidy that they'd actually been friends for the last year and she was truly invited to the wedding; the rest is all just another conniving way for Addison to hurt her sister or make herself look better on her wedding day.

Normally, I'm better than this, but my eyes can't help searching for Scarlett. When she finally does arrive, it's at the end of the last song.

This one is about losing love, then gaining another. Her eyes meet mine briefly as Adrian loops his arm through hers.

The priest.

Did I literally just lose to a priest over a misperception? Over my own fear? I keep playing and sing about moving on, and I want to scream into the microphone that the last thing on my mind is moving on. She ducks her head and smiles at a guest. Her parents approach and each gives her a hug and point at me, most likely saying how happy they are about the ceremony.

God only knows if I'll still be here by that time.

I won't leave without telling her, though. That would be a dick move, and I don't think I would even recover from it.

I wonder if I'm the only person that sometimes lives in their own imagination, singing or listening to tracks and thinking about a future I know will never exist. In this specific one, it's me and Scarlett laughing, traveling, her backstage, having someone to come home to.

My thoughts choke me. I think about kids.

I squeeze my eyes shut and finish the song, then finally address the room. "Thanks for letting me perform. Congratulations to the happy couple."

I almost drop my guitar in an effort to hand it to one of the stagehands and quickly walk down the stairs, only to be completely blindsided by Cassidy.

"Hey." Her smile's warm, pretty like always. "Can we have that talk now?"

Is *no* an option? I let out a heavy sigh. "Yeah, but wait here one minute."

I leave her standing by the stage and rush over to Scarlett. "Give me ten minutes, then we talk. Is that okay?"

Adrian's eyebrows shoot up, and he crosses his arms.

Dustin's suddenly gone silent by his side. Ah good, he clearly has chosen sides in this scenario. He looks everywhere but toward me.

Scarlett's smile is wobbly; her eyes have tears in them. I want to explain everything, but I'm petrified the tears will be for an entirely different reason. Her answer is a small whisper, "Okay."

An exhale of relief passes through me. "Okay, good, okay, I won't be long, I promise. And then I'll tell you everything."

She nods, her smile falls, and then so does her head. I see one solitary tear drip from her eye and onto her cheek.

If murder was possible through eye contact, Adrian will have killed me. He's livid, and I know what he's thinking: *I lost to this guy and he's leaving the treasure behind?*

I'd want to kick my own ass too.

I do want to kick my own ass for even being in this stupid position, for being put here, for not dealing with my past, for just being a general failure in facing my demons.

Reaching out to touch Scarlett isn't a good idea right now, so I give her my back like I did a year ago, only this time, it's because I'm going to turn right back around in a few minutes, this time it isn't final.

Please, God, let it not be final.

She's not all right.

I'm not all right either.

Cassidy's by the stage, giving me a cheerful smile as I approach. She has her hand on her stomach. I smile, happy for her, and offer her my arm. "Okay, let's go talk, but I have a girl I kind of love that I need to get back to, so let's make it quick."

Her smile gets even wider. "My only advice, don't let her walk away from you, and don't walk away first because you're afraid she'll take the first step."

I stop walking.

She stops with me but doesn't meet my eyes. "I'm sorry."

"For what?" I whisper.

"Breaking us."

# TWENTY-SIX

## Scarlett

"**W**ant me to punch him in the throat?" Adrian asks in a voice that is way too calm. "I do know a guy who used to poison people for the mafia. Naturally, he's baptized now, but he knows his stuff." He nods to himself like that's a better plan. "Even have a fourth cousin who runs one of the crime families in Chicago. He's a politician. Even better, politicians can hide everything!" He slams his fist on the table, giving me a jolt and making Dustin spill his cake onto his shirt. "Whoops."

"Red velvet stains," Dustin says in a sad voice as the cake slowly falls in clumps down to his pants. "Ah, I'm reminded of last night when my balls needed ice, now they clearly need cake too. Must they take everything from me?"

Adrian leans over and whispers, "I think the mouse incident is still messing with his head." He pats Dustin's shoulder. "Do you have a form for something like this?

223

Where you talk to your dick, balls, and cake? If so, I can probably grab one for you."

Dustin glares up at him. "It's been a traumatic few days, all right? Make fun of me again and I'm finding ten Gus-Gusses and putting them in her bed!"

I gasp. "You wouldn't!"

"I WOULD!"

Laughter bubbles out of me for the first time in an hour. "Dustin, first off you're the one with the creepy mouse facts, second, you looked ready to shit your pants—"

His voice comes out an octave too high. "It was on my dick! I need that!"

"'Cause you use it so much?" Adrian asks under his breath.

Dustin stands, his pants are stained with red velvet, as is his shirt. "I use it all the time; I'll prove it to you!"

"We don't need to watch," I say politely. "And you have nothing to prove. I'm sure it's a great, um, dick."

"It is! I get compliments all the time. I even have a girlfriend back home."

Adrian bursts out laughing. "Do you have a picture of her? Is she from Canada, though? Like have you met her?"

"Is she mail order?" I join in. "From overseas looking for a green card?"

He lifts his chin. "She's beautiful, and she's waiting for me after I get out of this hellhole."

"But is she real?" Adrian specifies. "Oh, wait!" He snaps his fingers. "Are you into that whole AI girlfriend thing? Is that your kink?"

"You"—Dustin points a finger at him—"are the devil."

Adrian and I share a smile as Dustin storms off, probably

in search of more cake to smear on his pants and to print out more documents and find a picture of the girlfriend who probably does exist, poor thing.

I'm afraid to see how the conversation between Killian and Cassidy is going. They're still talking out by the vineyard, but they don't seem upset. If anything, she just keeps smiling at him.

Is that his baby? Am I crazy for thinking that? Are they still in love? Is she the one that left him or broke his heart? Was it the opposite way around? Is that why he left me and didn't contact me for a year? I have so many questions with answers I don't think I want to hear. I move to stand when Adrian tugs my arm down. "Sit, you don't know yet, and the worst thing you can do in any romance movie is to walk away assuming the worst. Let him speak his peace."

I snort. "Wow, this coming from the one who studied thou shall not kill but nearly murdered him last night?"

"He had sex with you." He hisses and takes a huge bite of cake, chewing furiously like he's chomping down on Killian. "I still want to strangle him, but he's actually a good guy and I like his taste in style." Frown lines etch themselves across his forehead. "Just don't tell him I said that."

Guys are idiots. "It's literally identical to yours. It's like you're these weird long lost Jekyll Hyde brothers or something."

"Ha!" He drops his fork and sobers. "Could be true. I was adopted."

A hushed pause drops between us. "I mean, that would be crazy." I look closer. I mean, they do have some similarities. "Nahhhh, but can you imagine?"

"No. Because that would mean you slept with two brothers." He laughs.

"Ewww!" I cover my ears. "Stop it, I don't like it."

"Oh, you loooved it last night, probably what attracted the mouse in the first place," he says sarcastically.

I hit him in the shoulder, then pull his ear when he doesn't stop laughing.

"Ow, ow, stop! I'm sorry, okay?"

I let him go and smile sweetly. "Better?"

He rubs his ear and grabs his fork again, then looks up.

Killian's walking over, tie off in his hand, his face grim and downturned, not the Killian I know or the one I'm used to at least.

"It's not looking good, coach." I stand and put a hand on Adrian's. "Promise you'll always be my best friend and buy me donuts."

He points his fork at me. "Don't forget throwing groceries at old ladies and burning Addison's house down just because we can."

I laugh even though my soul wants to cry. "I do love you."

"I love you too. It'll be fine. I promise." He kisses my hand. "And priests should keep their vows to their best friends."

"They should," I admit. "However, nobody will judge you if you ever decide that it isn't the life for you."

He looks down at the black table both. "I think I'd just judge myself."

"Nah, I'll just punch you every time you do."

"Oh good, that's encouraging. Go get the rockstar before he cries. He doesn't look so good." He gets up. "I'm off for more cake and to make sure Dustin isn't trying to find a fake girlfriend amongst the guests."

"May the force be with you." I salute him.

"You too." He winks.

I smooth down my green dress and try not to stare down at my nude heels as I walk toward Killian in the grass.

He holds out his hand.

How wonderful would it be to know that that gesture would lead to forever or at least potential when I think he's about to say goodbye.

I take it anyway. It's warm, strong.

He's still in his groomsman clothes that don't really fit, an open white shirt and navy slacks that hug his ass like they're about to explode. Damn it, Addison.

"Let's talk," he whispers.

We walk for a while until we're overlooking the river in one of the vineyards, sitting on a wooden bench that's so fairy tale-like I want to set it on fire.

It's the kind of bench people get proposed to on.

It's the kind of bench people find love on.

Not the kind of bench people leave you on when they give you their back and walk away forever while you stare at the beauty in front of you.

I hate this bench so hard.

"So…" My hands are really shaky, so I pull them away and clasp them together. I don't want him letting me down easy while holding my hand; it feels too sad.

"That was my ex, Cassidy." He isn't looking at me.

She even has a pretty name, and she looked so kind. I hate her, but she has a baby… I touch my own stomach briefly, not something I can possibly think of right now.

I might break if I do.

"Oh." I smile. What else can I say? Yeah, I know it is.

I heard my sister. "Well then, is this a happy thing?" I'm reaching, stretching.

He turns fully to me, his smile sad but intact. "She just reminded me of a few things, apologized, and I think I found some answers to things I needed, I think in our weakest moments we turn to selfishness, inward, instead of outward, because it's too painful to reach for help and get rejected if nobody offers it."

My throat closes. "Then I'm happy for you, that you got to be with her, rekindle or… talk."

He sighs and puts a hand on my thigh. If he pats it, I'm going to murder him. I don't need him to patronize my tears. "I'm willing to walk away—from you."

My eyes widen. Did he just say what I think he said? Did he just? Did he just? I can't see because my eyes blur so hard. I promised I wouldn't cry, but the tears just stream down my face.

He swipes them away. "Let me finish."

"Finish ripping my heart out? Look, I knew this was going to happen. I just, I just wasn't prepared, I told myself I was, I just need to breathe a bit, oh it's nice, very nice fresh air." I inhale twice and nearly pass out. "See? I'm fine, just—" I almost suck in a bug. "Great! See? Great, what were you saying?"

"I'm willing to walk away if this bothers you, if it breaks you, my past. I'm willing to walk away, no questions asked. I'm willing to be strong and not fail myself or you again. I don't want secrets between us, so I'm letting you know now that I need you to not say it's okay if it's not, I need you to just tell me your truth after I tell you mine."

"You're scaring me." I sit back down on the bench. He

sits next to me and reaches for my hand like it's the last time he'll be touching it, he rubs his thumb back and forth. "My parents' divorce was expected, but what wasn't expected was me getting sick."

I freeze. "What kind of sick?"

He's still not looking at me, but he is rubbing my hand. "I got Leukemia. My dad's a doctor, and they were able to try an extremely aggressive chemo, but there were... side effects of the drugs they gave me at such a young age. I mean, I was only fourteen."

My eyes fill with tears. "Is that why you—"

"Honestly, Scarlett, I wanted to leave everything behind, but I did really lose your messenger account, and I was so out of it with the drugs that by the time I was able to even really focus a few weeks later, I searched everywhere for it. My dad had gone through my things trying to help. I'm pretty sure he threw out anything he saw as random scraps of paper or trash."

I close my eyes. All this time. All this resentment. And he was sick. "I'm so sorry you had to go through that. I really am."

He finally glances to his right, briefly making eye contact with me, his lips drawn up into a sexy smile. "Don't be, I had the sexiest nurse treating me every day."

"You are literally asking to be hit right now."

His laughter is better than a hit. He kisses my hand. "Sorry, you just left the perfect opening in a really sad moment, so I had to take my chances."

"I'll give you the free pass."

He lifts my hand to his lips and kisses it again. "Good."

I'm going to savor those small kisses for the rest of my life.

The way his soft lips touch my skin, the feeling of knowing he means each and every one.

"So." He bites down on his lower lip, frowns, then fully turns toward me. "A side effect of the chemo was that when I was cancer-free and fully healed, we found out I was…" He looks away from me. "We found out that I would be sterile the rest of my life."

My stomach drops to my knees. "What?"

"I know, I know, and I kept it from Cassidy because her only dream was to be a mom. I just kept telling myself that it would be okay, we could adopt, it would be fine, my career was taking off and the busier I got the more I stopped wanting to tell her, which was selfish but she was by my side and I was afraid if I did say something she'd leave. One month her period was late, and she was so damn excited, she took a pregnancy test and like a fucking asshole I drove her to the stupid store and let her believe it could be true. I think the worst part is that when it was negative, I was like, oh good, at least she's not cheating. I mean, how horrible of a human being can you be? Really? I was young and stupid, but that's no excuse. She cried that night, and when I told her that it was fine, that if we couldn't get pregnant, we'd just adopt or foster, she looked up at me like I'd just killed parts of her soul. She said she wanted to carry a baby, she'd always wanted to carry a baby. Just like it was my dream to sing, hers had always been to carry her own child." Tears flow down my face. "The band got more and more famous, and she was on the road with us a lot. She ended up getting extremely close with one of my bandmates, Hudson. It made me jealous. I was the lead singer, he was one of the main dancers and did mostly backup, so he had more time on his hands. They started going out on excursions, and while I didn't care, part of me did, because he could give her what I couldn't."

I truly can't believe he's telling me all of this right now.

Killian's knee starts to bounce up and down. "So, one night, she comes home and says she missed her period again, and I freaked out. I fucking lost my mind and said she was cheating." He starts to choke up. "She was so confused, so hurt I would lash out at her, so I just blurted out that I was sterile from my chemo and that if she was pregnant, she was cheating. We got into a huge fight, and she left me that night, no explanation, blocked my phone. I knew Hudson was still in contact with her. And sure enough. About a month later, maybe two, the band broke up, and she started dating him." His voice cracks. "They're expecting their first child, as you so clearly saw." He nods his head, tears run down his cheeks. "So, there you go, that's it, that's why I didn't tell you. I was weak, afraid, just like I am now, I was a complete ass to her, but I'm happy for them, I really am. I'm sad that the band broke up because of my own inability to hold my shit together on top of us wanting to go our own directions, but at least they're happy. I think I can find a bit of solace in that."

I'm so stunned I can barely move. In all the secrets I thought he had, most of them included secret babies, drug usage, prison—nothing had anything to do with what he just confessed.

Slowly, I let go of his hand and stand to face him. "I'll walk away. If you want me to, I'll walk away."

He jerks his head up, tears still streaming down his face. "What?"

"If you want me to, I'll walk away, but only after my turn."

"Your turn?"

"You see…" I hold my hands out in front of me, squeezing them together. "We all have secrets. When I was with Rob, I had a miscarriage, which caused me to have to go to the doctor, which also caused several examinations, which ended up explaining why I miscarried. My chances, after having the walls of my uterus painfully scraped when they discovered that I had the onset of uterine cancer, meant my chances of conceiving were less than one percent even if I took treatment." I shrug. "Rob didn't take the news well, you know, because it's important to have someone with your bloodline." I laugh. "He literally said that to me as I was holding my knees to my stomach crying from the pain and humiliation of staring a nurse down while she looked back at me like it was my fault, when I had nothing to do with it. My body rebelled, it's as simple as that." I swipe the tears from my own cheeks. "So, I'm telling you the same thing. If the broken you wants the broken me to walk away, I will, no questions asked, but Killian, I really, really, want you to ask me to stay."

He jumps to his feet and pulls me into his embrace so tight that I can barely breathe. "It's not your fault."

"It's not yours either," I whisper back, holding him so close I feel his pain wrap around me like a blanket. Suffocating both of us, freeing us at the same time.

"Stay." His lips move across my neck. "Please stay with me. Please don't go."

"If I stay, you stay." We pull away from each other, I reach up and wipe the wetness from his cheeks. "You're perfect the way you are. Plus, we do have Dustin to raise, so…"

He bursts out laughing and rests his head against mine. "Might need to hire a nanny."

"Maybe if we get him into organized sports?"

"Just not rugby, he'd die," Killian agrees.

"Checkers could be a consideration. He can wear his bow ties, make some sickass moves with his hands, hey and I bet they have documents he can sign, he'll probably cry." I giggle and grab Killian's collar. "Now, can you please kiss me and then fake marry me tomorrow?"

His smile falls.

"What? What's wrong? More secrets? Oh no, you have a mistress?" I look around. "We're on camera? Your agent's pissed again?"

Killian drops to his knee and looks up at me. "A year ago, you asked me to sing for you. Today, I only have one question."

My heart stops.

"Scarlett, will you marry me?"

# TWENTY-SEVEN

*Killian*

**S**carlett's eyes go wide.

I have no ring.

No special words.

Only one question.

"I'll marry you!" Shouts Adrian from the right.

I shoot him a glare. "Kinda busy here, Adrian."

"No, not that." He winks at me. "I mean, I'll *marry* you guys. I *am* a priest, so I can get the job done and we can do the official paperwork when you two get back. I'm sure Dustin has a guy for that."

Dustin rushes up, stained with cake all over his pants and shirt. "Were you in a war I wasn't aware of?" I ask.

"Oh." He waves me off. "Addison and Rob got in another fight about cheating, I walked right in the middle after searching for more cake, Gertrude got drunk again, one of the guests fell on the buffet table… It's been a gas!" He

looks ready to pass out. "Anyway, I do have a guy; I have a guy for everything. Why am I contacting a guy? Hey, why are you on your knee?" You can literally see the moment his math finally works out. "Are you proposing?"

"Yes!" Scarlett yells. "And you're interrupting!"

Dustin starts patting his pants weirdly, then starts to pull out a folded piece of paper.

"Ruin this and I will set you on fire and watch you roll down the hill burning down the entire winery," I snap.

Slowly, he gulps and continues to pull out the piece of paper. "Actually, um, I was going to say, I carried an extra copy of the wedding certificate for Addison to sign and send in so she would stop yelling at people, I kept it in my pocket during the ceremony, so technically, we do have paperwork, since this one can marry you, we just need to register it when we get home. When will that be? Never? Do we even have a home anymore? Time, it moves so slow here." He looks up at the sun like he's telling time, then stares back at us. "Oh sorry, continue."

Scarlett smiles down at me. "Definitely not football."

"Never."

We both burst out laughing. She pulls me to my feet and wraps her arms around my neck. "I want a rockstar ring."

"Oh, greedy already?"

She nods. "Yeah, and I know what shape I want it in."

"I like a woman who knows what she wants."

"You think they can find a ring that looks like a star?"

I search her eyes waiting for an explanation.

"Because the other night I wished on one, didn't work though, so I just wished on you. Maybe that could be my ring, a reminder that wishing on the man did the job, and the star sealed the fate?"

"God, I love you." I lift her into my arms and kiss her as hard as I can. She stumbles backward as our mouths collide.

Adrian whispers, "I now pronounce you man and wife."

We break apart and gape at him.

"Oh, please." He rolls his eyes. "I wouldn't sell you short like that, but I mean, it really is that easy." Screaming ensues from the reception. "Better idea, let's go steal some wine and go somewhere quiet."

I grab Scarlett's hand and kiss it, then I hold it the entire way through the chaos of the drunken reception, with all of the groomsmen fighting, bridesmaids crying, Addison accusing, parents watching on like they don't know where it went wrong, and the rest of us misfits stealing more champagne and wine, getting ready for our big day.

One that will be real.

# TWENTY-EIGHT

## Scarlett

"**P**aradise," he whispers, thrusting into me. "Maybe I'll just live like this for a while, inside you, pleasing you, teasing you." His mouth moves down my ass, his fingers part my thighs. I squirm as a warm tongue slides up and down. Firm hands keep me steady, then move me from the table, bent over, to the wall. He pins me there and holds me hostage with his body, and I crave every minute of it, each stroke, each wet kiss. He'd sent me to bed, only to wake me up hours later, already inside me. He took me from behind twice before breakfast, and when I woke up.

I jolt awake and shake my head. What time is it? I'm still in bed but Killian's gone, maybe he got hungry because after last night everything became a blur. It was a ton of wine and laughter, followed by a ton of late-night sex, which I'm sure traumatized the guys, but they were probably too drunk to notice.

I rub my eyes and fully sit up, and on the pillow is a note. I open it quickly.

"Eat breakfast and get ready, you have a groom waiting for you in the front vineyard at noon."

I check the clock. I have exactly two hours to get ready. I stumble out of bed, catch my feet on the comforter and go flying toward the carpeted floor, scramble up, and dash into the bathroom without knocking.

Adrian's naked in the shower and Dustin's on the toilet.

I cover my eyes with my hands. "Do I even want to know?"

Dustin flushes and stands, yanking his boxers up. "Wine does not agree with me, and Adrian had no choice unless he wanted to come out. He's been in there for a while just humming to himself." Dustin starts laughing and stumbles toward the sink. "I think I'm still drunk."

"Ya think?" Adrian yells. "I had to witness this!"

"You're a priest! You've seen worse!"

"Have I? Have I?" Adrian roars.

Dustin laughs to himself. "We're probably best friends now."

"I rebuke you in the name of—" He starts screaming. "Ahhh, scalding, scalding, why did it get so hot?"

I sigh and lean against the door. "Grab a towel, it's my turn."

Adrian turns off the shower, I don't watch but hear his movements. "Not like you haven't seen me naked before."

"Yes and you were so impressed by my nakedness you went to the cloth." I giggle. "You got everything covered, big guy?"

"Yes," he grumbles. "I hate Dustin and yet I want to keep him around, but maybe if we had a leash, you know?" He grabs a toothbrush.

I shake my head at him in the mirror. "He just needs a bit of training."

Adrian rolls his eyes. "How did he become this way, I wonder?"

"Oh, that's easy. Killian said Dustin's an Emory, as in Max Emory's cousin. I think it was Max who drove him this way. He used to work at Emory Enterprises full time before he was offered an escape and went over to the agency. Killian said he cried the first day at work, but not because he was sad, so I'm going to guess that's the reason?"

"Wow." Adrian shakes his head. "Full circle. I heard that guy was one of those brilliant lunatics. Can't imagine working for him."

Dustin pokes his head back in the bathroom. "Don't imagine it, you'll manifest it."

He closes the door, leaving us alone.

Adrian finishes up and takes his toothbrush. "All yours. Oh!" He points his toothbrush at me. "And Killian said to wear the white dress in your closet."

"What white dress?" I ask.

Adrian gives me a dumbfounded look. "Um, I'm not sure, Scar, I don't exactly go through your closet. Oh, and Chuck tried escaping last night, but Mrs. Junger just tucked him back in with some beef. I think she texted you, but you were…" His cheeks turn pink. "Very, very, very, very, a billion times very, busy."

"Shut up." I feel myself blushing. "I'm going to take a quick shower."

"Yes hedonist, you do that."

He's gone before I can throw something at him.

'm sluggish but ready in no time after Adrian brings me coffee. I keep telling myself I'm crazy, but I've done things the normal way. This just seems like the way it was supposed to go the whole time.

My wedding to a rockstar.

No, my wedding to the man I love, Killian Stone.

When I finally go to my closet to put on my dress, I do see a white one hanging there. It's a silvery white, and has a slit completely up the side, the train pools around my feet. In a Grecian style, it ties with an embellished knot at the waist before coming up to a structured strapless top with tiny crystals sewn in.

How did he even get this here on time?

There's a bag attached to it with a gorgeous gray corset and matching thong and inside of that is a box.

I open it quickly and find two silver bands; they're simple but beautiful. My smile gets bigger when I see silver heels in the same bag.

"How did he do this?" I make a mental note to ask him later: when did he do this?

I briefly remember him leaving when we got back to the room, but it was at least six at night, and the closest designer you can get is probably Seattle?

Can you even overnight ship that late?

I smile down at the dress and put on everything as carefully as possible, then walk out to see the guys.

They're both dressed in gray slacks and off-white shirts with silver ties. They look incredible.

Seriously, when did he do this?

Adrian smiles over at me. "I know your mind's spinning right now, not from the wine but from the surprises, so just bask in the fact that your fiancé thought of everything."

I nod so I don't burst into tears, then whisper. "Can you zip me?"

"Cruel woman." He grins. "Turn around."

His hands are warm and firm as he zips up my dress and kisses the back of my head. "Perfect, best friend, just perfect."

I turn and hold out both hands to them. "All right, let's do this."

# TWENTY-NINE

## *Killian*

I called my agent the minute we got back to the house, broke the news, threatened to fire her, then after she calmed down and realized I was serious, she helped me get a courier to drive all the way from Seattle with the clothes, shoes, lingerie, and rings.

It wasn't cheap, but we did offer them a free overnight stay plus all expenses paid on top of double their hourly rate. They were more than happy to make the nearly four-hour trip.

I'm more nervous right now than I was playing sold-out shows all over the world. I think I might actually puke.

What if she changes her mind?

What if she does walk away?

What if this isn't real?

"Need a little of this?" Karen, aka Kitty, offers me her champagne glass.

I laugh. "No, I think I can do it without champagne."

"The question is not if you can, the question is, do you want to?" She winks. "You'll be just fine, I'll be over there with my ball and chain."

"Good to know." She's literally going to move two feet away from me, not to Siberia. She's hilarious, though, I'll give her that.

The only people present are her parents. Addison, of course, said she had a headache after the fights from last night.

Good fucking riddance.

I'm glad Adrian listened to me. He walks up the hill and waves, Bible in hand, and meets me at the front with Dustin. "Ready?"

I nod a few times. "Might hurl, but sure, yeah."

"Remember, she did puke on you."

"Revenge, a dish best served… wet?" Dustin frowns. "Yeah, that doesn't work, all right, so I'm just going to be standing over here filming—"

"Nope, got that covered." I grab him by the collar. "You're a groomsman, you both are, though Adrian might need a little help with the vow part."

He laughs. "Got you covered."

Adrian looks around. "It's so nice and quiet."

"Like a dream, seriously." Dustin snorts. "But do we have any music for her to walk out to?"

"Be right back, wish me luck."

I jog down the hill and find my bride. Her back's to me, but it's not because she's turning away.

No, it's because she's waiting for me.

Funny how my entire life I thought about that gesture

as leaving, and recently of Cassidy giving me her back, and now I see my bride doing the same, but she's doing it with patience, not regret, betrayal, or anger.

And from what I see, the dress is stunning.

I hired one of the videographers to film everything and may have conned three teens vacationing here into doing some TikToks for me. I paid them a hundred bucks each, they'll survive.

"You ready, beautiful?"

Scarlett looks over her shoulder. Her makeup is light, her lips pink, her hair pulled into a low ponytail, with pieces falling away from it. The dress fits her perfectly, like it was sculpted for her. It trails behind her as she slowly walks toward me, eyes blinking slowly as she takes me in and laughs. "Are you seriously wearing leather pants right now, all your rockstar jewelry, and a gray T-shirt?"

"Your fault." I hold out my hand. "You texted Leather Pants to rescue you, and now we rescue each other. It's only natural that I'd show up like the true rockstar."

She loops her arm in mine. "You look sexy."

I capture her mouth in a hungry kiss and pull away. "And you look stunning."

She leans her head on my shoulder as we walk up the hill, and without any sort of background music, I start to sing.

God Bless the Broken Road.

I begin the first verse, then get choked up, and nearly stop singing. She looks up at me, and I look down at her and continue. "...Others who broke my heart, they were like northern stars..." I sing the entire way to the front and face her parents.

Adrian clears his throat. "Who gives this woman to this man?"

Her dad smiles warmly at us. "Her mother and I do."

We walk past them, hand in hand, to the front, facing Adrian. I know it's bittersweet, but I also know that I wouldn't want anyone else at this point to be the person helping us with our vows.

"Killian, you said to keep it simple, and honestly I know in my soul this will be the last time I have to stand before your bride and ask her to read her vows, though let's hope this time they aren't—" He stops talking at my glare. He clears his throat. "Scarlett, do you take Killian to be your loving husband, to be with you through sickness and in health, through hard times, and good, stand by his side until the end?"

"Yes," she says it so quickly I almost do a double take. Did she really *really* say yes?

"And Killian do you—"

"Yes, just yes, I'll take her turtle to the vet if he gets sick, I'll walk the dog with the blind eye, I'll buy her flowers just because she likes the way they look, and I swear, I'll sing to her every single time she asks, until the end. I'll sing to her until the very end."

Scarlett's ruining her makeup with her tears, but it just makes her look prettier. Dustin reaches into his pocket and hands the bands to Adrian.

"Rings are a symbol of eternity, of forever," he says. "Stay by each other's side, no matter what, be the symbol you wear." He hands Scarlett the ring, she holds it to my left hand and looks up while sliding it on.

It fits.

We fit.

Adrian hands me her ring. I hold it to her left hand and lean in, kissing her while I slip it on. I don't even hear what Adrian says.

"Um," Adrian clears his throat, we don't stop kissing. "By the power vested in me by—" He sighs. "May I now present Mr. and Mrs. Killian Stone. You may continue kissing your bride."

There are only a few claps.

If there were a million, I wouldn't hear them.

Because my only focus is her.

She may have exposed the groom a year ago—but I'm the lucky one that stole the bride.

# EPILOGUE

## Killian

"No." I shake my head and kiss down her neck. She's naked, I'm naked, it's perfect. We're on our honeymoon in Portugal, and she found a turtle, decided it was a good idea to get Chuck a friend. "He already has the two dogs and the cat from the winery that you adopted before we left for the honeymoon."

She flips me over onto my back, shimmies herself onto my dick, and starts to move slowly. Shit, she knows what this does to me.

I can't think straight.

Am I slurring my words or just my thoughts?

Why is the sky blue?

Fuck.

"Killian…" She moves slow, deep. What even is life right now? "Don't you think Chuck is lonely? He's all by himself."

"Yes." I grip her by the hips and move her up and down,

harder, faster. "Yes, so lonely, loneliness sucks." Ah so close, she clenches around me. I bite down on my lower lip, nearly drawing blood as she leans down and licks around my ear, only to cool it with her mouth and kiss down my neck with more nibbles. Then she moves back and reaches around her ass and cups my balls.

I jolt forward and sit up as she rides me.

"I mean…" Manipulative woman. "He would be small, we can handle one more."

"We can handle everything, just don't stop."

She stops and grins up at me. "Hmm?"

"What? What fresh hell?" I grip her by the ass and, still inside her, flip her onto her stomach. "You'll definitely pay for that."

I screw her long and hard, thinking of it like a punishment when really, I'm enjoying the way her body responds.

"Killian," she moans. "We were having a conversation."

"It was…" I groan and pump into her again. "… completely one sided."

"No."

"Yes." I slap her ass. "Oh, yes."

I'm exhausted seconds later and collapse next to her.

"Thank you so much!" She kisses me on the mouth.

"For sex?" Did I pass out for a minute? Never had an orgasm do that to me before.

"You said oh yes at the end when I asked one more time. What do you think we should name him?"

I groan into my hands. "MC Hammer. Every turtle needs a sidekick."

"Brilliant." She high fives my abs. "Ready for round three?"

"No." I shove her away. "You weaponized sex for a turtle!"

"And you hated it so much?" She laughs and ruffles my hair. "Let's go, we'll be late for lunch with Adrian."

"Can't believe he came to our honeymoon," I grumble, getting off the bed.

"Dustin did invite him ever since he took a sabbatical and you know how bored he was, he wouldn't stop texting you reels and TikToks, so technically it's your fault you invited him to the honeymoon aka your European tour."

I laugh. "Hey, having a chaplain on the road for a rock tour, there really is a first for everything."

"I especially like how the backup dancers hit on him every single concert." She wraps her arms around me. "I love you."

I kiss her on the head. "I love you too." After slapping her ass, I go and get ready.

For the first time, I'm not alone on the road. I truly have a family, though I'll die before telling Dustin that. Ever since the wedding, my popularity skyrocketed. I'd like to thank TikTokkers everywhere for that.

I go into the bathroom and smile into the mirror when a knock sounds at the door.

"I'll get it!" Scarlett calls.

She opens it and chaos ensues.

"You guys are always late to brunch!" Adrian complains. "And you promised mimosas after you lost the turtle bet."

"Oh, leave it!" Scarlett yells. "It was one race on the beach, and you can't cheat by throwing sand in my turtle's way."

I laugh and spit out the toothpaste, then stare at myself in the mirror. This is my life, listening to friends argue about turtle races before going on stage, dancing around and looking as sexy as humanly possible.

Dustin suddenly appears at the door and knocks. "Yo, I gotta use the toilet. They have so much wine here, I just can't say no."

"Learn how," I bite out. "And yeah, just don't forget to wash your hands."

"I never forget."

I stare him down.

He grumbles, "It was one time, and I was drunk."

"Use soap," I remind him, then shut the door and lean against it while Adrian and Scarlett continue to argue. Now it's about watering house plants.

It never ends with this crew.

And I know, I'll never see someone's back again, unless they're mooning me, running for safety after a nerf race, or chasing a stalker that's trying to follow me.

Life is good.

Hey, maybe you should just take your chances when they're thrown at you, and maybe if you have a cheating bastard of a partner, you expose the shit out of them and move to greener pastures.

Then, by all means.

Buy a fucking turtle.

# CAUGHT YOU!

*Did you catch the name drops?*

Zane Andrews was supposed to be the musician at
Addison's wedding.
Curious about his story?
Meet **Zane** in his book *Keep, a Seaside Pictures Novel*.

Dustin's cousin is Max Emory.
Curious about their stories?
Meet **Max** in the *Consequence Series*.
Meet **Dustin** in *The Emory Games Series*.

And finally our mafia politician, Chase Abandonato.
Curious about his story?
Meet **Chase** in his books *Entice & Eulogy*!

# WANT MORE RVD?

Did you enjoy EXposing The Groom?
Then check out these other Romantic Comedies!

### THE BET SERIES
*New Adult, Romantic Comedies—Interconnected Standalones*
*The Bet (Travis & Kacey's story)*
*The Wager (Jake & Char Lynn's story)*
*The Dare (Jace & Beth Lynn's story)*

### THE CONSEQUENCE SERIES
*New Adult, Laugh Out Loud Romantic Comedies—Interconnected Standalones*
*The Consequence of Loving Colton (Colton & Milo's story)*
*The Consequence of Revenge (Max & Becca's story)*
*The Consequence of Seduction (Reid & Jordan's story)*
*The Consequence of Rejection (Jason & Maddy's story)*

### LIARS, INC
*New Adult, Romantic Comedies—Interconnected Standalones*
*Dirty Exes (Colin, Jessie & Blaire's story)*
*Dangerous Exes (Jessie & Isla's story)*

# ACKNOWLEDGMENTS

Thanks was truly a labor of love for all of my readers.

Thank you so much to Jill for carrying this entire release for me.

Again, I'm so thankful to God I get to do what I love every day.

Thank you to my family for allowing me to write this and work on it during the busy baseball season.

Can't wait to write more.

You can follow me on Facebook, Instagram, and TikTok.

HUGS

*rvd*

# ABOUT THE AUTHOR

**R**achel Van Dyken is the #1 *New York Times*, *Wall Street Journal*, and *USA Today* bestselling author of over 100 books, ranging from new adult romance to mafia romance to paranormal & fantasy romance. With over four million copies sold, she's been featured in *Forbes*, *US Weekly*, and *USA Today*. Her books have been translated into more than 15 countries. She was one of the first romance authors to have a Kindle in Motion book through Amazon publishing and continues to strive to be on the cutting edge of the reader experience. She keeps her home in the Pacific Northwest with her husband, adorable sons, naked cat, and two dogs. For more information about her books and upcoming events, visit www.RachelVanDykenAuthor.com.

# ALSO BY RACHEL VAN DYKEN

**Eagle Elite**
*New Adult, Mafia Romance — Interconnected Standalones*
*Elite (Nixon & Trace's story)*
*Elect (Nixon & Trace's story)*
*Entice (Chase & Mil's story)*
*Elicit (Tex & Mo's story)*
*Bang Bang (Axel & Amy's story)*
*Enforce (Elite+ from the boys' POV)*
*Ember (Phoenix & Bee's story)*
*Elude (Sergio & Andi's story)*
*RIP: A Bratva Brotherhood Novel (Nikolai & Maya's story)*
*Empire (Sergio & Val's story)*
*Enrage (Dante & El's story)*
*Eulogy (Chase & Luciana's story)*
*Exposed (Dom & Tanit's story)*
*Envy (Vic & Renee's story)*
*Debase: A Bratva Brotherhood Novel (Andrei & Alice's story)*
*Dissolution (Santino & Katya's story)*

## Cruel Summer Trilogy
### *New Adult, Angsty Romance — Trilogy*
*Summer Heat (Marlon & Ray's story)*
*Summer Seduction (Marlon & Ray's story)*
*Summer Nights (Marlon & Ray's story)*

## Ruin Series
### *Upper Young Adult/New Adult, Angsty Romances —*
### *Interconnected Standalones*
*Ruin (Wes Michels & Kiersten's story)*
*Toxic (Gabe Hyde & Saylor's story)*
*Fearless (Wes Michels & Kiersten's story)*
*Shame (Tristan & Lisa's story)*

## Seaside Series
### *Young Adult, Angsty, Rockstar Romances —*
### *Interconnected Standalones*
*Tear (Alec, Demetri & Natalee's story)*
*Pull (Demetri & Alyssa's story)*
*Shatter (Alec & Natalee's story)*
*Forever (Alec & Natalee's story)*
*Fall (Jamie Jaymeson & Pricilla's story)*
*Strung (Tear+ from the boys' POV)*
*Eternal (Demetri & Alyssa's story)*

## Seaside Pictures
### *New Adult, Dramedy (RomCom with Dramatic Moments),*
### *Rockstar/Movie Star Romances — Interconnected Standalones*
*Capture (Lincoln & Dani's story)*
*Keep (Zane & Fallon's story)*
*Steal (Will & Angelica's story)*
*All Stars Fall (Trevor & Penelope's story)*
*Abandon (Ty & Abigail's story)*
*Provoke (Braden & Piper's story)*
*Surrender (Drew & Bronte's story)*

## Standalone Romances
### *New Adult, Angsty Romance — Standalone Novels*
*The Perfects (Ambrose & Mary-Belle's story)*
*The Unperfects (Quinn's story)*

## Players Game
### *New Adult, Sports Romances — Interconnected Standalones*
*Fraternize (Miller, Grant and Emerson's story)*
*Infraction (Miller & Kinsey's story)*
*M.V.P. (Jax & Harley's story)*

## Covet
### *New Adult, Angsty Romances — Interconnected Standalones*
*Stealing Her (Bridge & Isobel's story)*
*Finding Him (Julian & Keaton's story)*

## The Bet Series
### *New Adult, RomComs — Interconnected Standalones*
*The Bet (Travis & Kacey's story)*
*The Wager (Jake & Char Lynn's story)*
*The Dare (Jace & Beth Lynn's story)*

## The Bachelors of Arizona
### *New Adult Romances — Interconnected Standalones*
*The Bachelor Auction (Brock & Jane's story)*
*The Playboy Bachelor (Bentley & Margot's story)*
*The Bachelor Contract (Brant & Nikki's story)*

## The Consequence Series
### *New Adult, Laugh Out Loud RomComs —*
### *Interconnected Standalones*
*The Consequence of Loving Colton (Colton & Milo's story)*
*The Consequence of Revenge (Max & Becca's story)*
*The Consequence of Seduction (Reid & Jordan's story)*
*The Consequence of Rejection (Jason & Maddy's story)*

**London Fairy Tales**
*Fairy Tale Inspired Regency Romances — Interconnected Standalones*
*Upon a Midnight Dream (Stefan & Rosalind's story)*
*Whispered Music (Dominique & Isabelle's story)*
*The Wolf's Pursuit (Hunter & Gwendolyn's story)*
*When Ash Falls (Ashton & Sofia's story)*

**Renwick House**
*Regency Romances — Interconnected Standalones*
*The Ugly Duckling Debutante (Nicholas & Sara's story)*
*The Seduction of Sebastian St. James (Sebastian & Emma's story)*
*The Redemption of Lord Rawlings (Phillip & Abigail's story)*
*An Unlikely Alliance (Royce & Evelyn's story)*
*The Devil Duke Takes a Bride (Benedict & Katherine's story)*

# EXPOSING THE GROOM CONTAINS:

EXposing the Groom is a laugh-out-loud RomCom that touches on a few real life topics.

CHEATING: The only cheating in the book is what is expressed in the blurb. The two main characters are faithful throughout the book.

CANCER: is briefly mentioned as part of the backstory.

www.rachelvandykenauthor.com